"I want to thank you for a wonderful evening. One I've needed for a long, long time," Blain said.

"I find that rather hard to believe," Bobbi replied, practically gulping. Her eyes found it easier to rest on his evening-shadow chin instead of the all too penetrating blue eyes studying her face, her lips, in such an intimate measure. "I thought this night would have been routine for you."

"And why would you think that?" His hand traveled along the side of her neck, his thumb tracing slow, nerve-tingling circles just below her ear.

"Surely you don't expect me to believe you lead a celibate life, Mr. Pearson."

In response, Blain's free hand covered one of Bobbi's breasts and began a sensuous, drugging massage like none other Bobbi had ever experienced....

Dear Reader,

It is our pleasure to bring you a new experience in reading that goes beyond category writing. The settings of **Harlequin American Romance** give a sense of place and culture that is uniquely American, and the characters are warm and believable. The stories are of "today" and have been chosen to give variety within the vast scope of romance fiction.

Jessica Jeffries's first novel is like a basketball game, which is indeed the core of this book. The hero and heroine take many time-outs. Bobbi doesn't score any points with Blain when she has his car repossessed, but Blain rebounds quickly, as his offensive strategy surprises her.

From the early days of Harlequin, our primary concern has been to bring you novels of the highest quality. **Harlequin American Romance** is no exception. Enjoy!

Vivian Stephens

Vivian Stephens
Editorial Director
Harlequin American Romance
919 Third Avenue,
New York, N.Y. 10022

All in the Game

JESSICA JEFFRIES

Harlequin Books

TORONTO • NEW YORK • LONDON
AMSTERDAM • PARIS • SYDNEY • HAMBURG
STOCKHOLM • ATHENS • TOKYO • MILAN

Published September 1983

First printing July 1983

ISBN 0-373-16022-4

Chapter One

Easy pickin's, thought Bobbi, eyeing the sleek silver Corvette arrogantly parked across the dividing stripe, taking up a full two spaces of the crowded parking lot. A smug grin lifted the corners of her mouth as she lowered the window of her car and signaled to the driver of the wrecker following her. With a nod he gunned the motor of the truck and pulled up ahead of her past the Corvette. Within seconds he had backed up, positioning the truck sufficiently to hook the sports car onto his rig.

Bobbi stepped out of her car, walked briskly to the Corvette, and unlocked the door with the specially prepared key, then slid inside to adjust the gears. As the driver of the wrecker went about the mechanics of mounting the vehicle, Bobbi returned to her car, removing her wallet from her purse to extract the cash payment for his services.

"That was fast, Mike," Bobbi commended the driver, handing the burly young man his due. "You're getting faster and better every time."

"If you handled ten of these jobs a day the way I do, you'd be fast, too." Mike accepted the money and shoved it into a back pocket of his grubby jeans, opening the cab door of his truck and heaving his lumbering, husky build inside.

"I guess so." Bobbi chuckled, lifting a hand to shade her eyes from the harsh glare of the afternoon sun. "I'll give you a call the next time."

Mike winked, then spit expertly onto the tarmac. "Sure thing." He waved a meaty hand as he gunned the motor, setting off through the crowded section of the Capital Centre's enormous parking area, mindless of the expensive sports car he was pulling along behind him. All in a day's work to him, Bobbi mused, walking back to her tiny economical Toyota.

And, she thought smugly, all in a day's work for herself. Well, not quite, she admitted, pushing the keys into the ignition and backing out, maneuvering the car in the same direction as Mike's wrecker, though with considerably less haste. That particular skip trace had taken a good deal more effort on her part than most others, but persistence had paid off, and right there in the Washington, D.C. area, at that. She couldn't have wished for a more satisfying conclusion to her efforts of the past six months than to be able to personally handle the repossession of Mr. Blain Pearson's expensive toy—no doubt one of many such pleasant amenities of his extremely lucrative career. Professional basketball players were supposedly the highest paid among athletes, Bobbi understood, and it was that factor more than anything that had fueled her normally powerful investigative instincts to even stronger efforts.

It irked her to think that a person of Blain Pearson's

financial status would even think of reneging on a loan for a car. Why, he could probably have paid cash for it, she seethed, thinking how hard it was for her to keep up the payments on her Toyota. Not that she was destitute—she managed to support herself quite well. Her time with AMAC finance company had paid off in the long run, much to her satisfaction, but there again persistence had paid off. Her position as credit representative had expanded during the last year and a half, encompassing the challenging and oftentimes exciting job requirements of a skip tracer.

Bobbi had discovered that she had a definite bent for such investigative work. It had come along at just the right time, when interest in her normal duties was beginning to wane and the thought of finding another job, albeit at a lower salary, was starting to look more appealing every day. The new position, however, had soon become all-consuming, her duties as credit representative fading to nonexistence. In addition, AMAC had rewarded Bobbi's efforts with a monetary bonus that made thoughts of switching jobs downright impractical at that point and, after such a rewarding day as it had been, almost traitorous.

"So, how did it go?"

Bobbi glanced up from her preoccupation with the folder she was thumbing through to see Ralph Goodman peering around the doorway of her office, his lanky brown hair falling onto his forehead as carelessly as the black-rimmed glasses perched precariously on the tip of his nose. "Did you finally catch up with our renowned basketball star?"

Bobbi chuckled and shoved her own pair of reading glasses back up the pert length of her nose, running one hand alongside her neck to free the mass of thick cinnamon-brown tresses that had slipped over her shoulders and onto the front of her tangerine sweater. She was amused with Ralph's unflagging interest in the latest of her conquests of delinquent accounts. Sometimes she thought he rather envied the excitement and challenge inherent in her position, so different from his own routine job in the accounting department.

"As a matter of fact, yes," Bobbi answered. "I was just going over the illustrious Blain Pearson's file. You know, it's amazing that someone so financially secure would be so ignorant as to ruin his credit by defaulting on his loan. It just doesn't make sense."

Ralph lifted his eyebrows and turned down the corners of his mouth as he shrugged. "Happens to the best of us, you know. What the heck, maybe he has an ex-wife and kids to support. And the amount those guys have to pay their agents is pretty hefty, from what I hear. By the time the poor guy gets through supporting all his hangers-on he probably does have a hard time making ends meet."

"Aw, come on, Ralph. You and I make it through life on considerably less. And without getting into financial trouble." She paused and tapped her finger on the desk. "And I know for a fact that he doesn't have a wife."

"Well, I suppose you do have a point," Ralph conceded. "But where's your heart, lady? Don't you ever wonder what the poor guy's gonna do when he discovers his car has been snatched right out from under his nose? Where did you pick it up anyway?''

"At the Capital Centre. The Bullets are in town for a game against the Lakers this weekend.''

"That's right.'' Ralph nodded. "The Bullets are favored.''

Bobbi shrugged dismissively. "I for one couldn't care less about who wins. Basketball is not exactly my favorite sport. But,'' she added with a sly smirk, "this game's the very one I've been waiting for. He had to come home sometime. It was just a matter of waiting for the proper moment to move in for the kill.''

Ralph's expression indicated his admiration for Bobbi's cunning technique. "That's right. His home is in these parts, isn't it? Somewhere in Maryland or Virginia?''

"Mmm-mm. Fairfax, Virginia. That's where he's originally from. Although, as far as I've discovered, the man doesn't really have a home. He spends so much time traveling around the country, I can't imagine how he'd have time for a family.''

"Doesn't sound like it,'' Ralph agreed. Glancing at his watch, he stood and said, "Well, I've gotta run.'' He lifted one hand to his forehead in mock salute. "Talk to you later, Detective Morrows.''

Bobbi grinned absently and glanced back down at the folder virtually stuffed with information pertaining to the professional basketball player's whereabouts for the previous six months. Strange, she mused, she almost regretted having finally solved the case. She had enjoyed it more than any she'd worked on till then. Blain Pearson's life was nothing if not interesting. She had to hand it to the man. Even though unable to handle his finances, he managed to live an enviable life by most people's standards. Assuming, of course, that one enjoyed playing professional basketball for a living.

Basketball, Bobbi thought, shaking her head ruefully. The one sport about which she cared absolutely nothing—until then, of course. Her determination to solve the case, an accomplishment that could only improve her increasingly successful record, had forced her to set aside her prejudices for the time. But it was a sacrifice well worth making. She was satisfied for the meantime with her promotion from credit rep to skip tracer, but that was only another rung on the ladder she intended to climb on her way out of the middle-management trap.

The following afternoon as Bobbi was returning from lunch she passed the switchboard operator's desk, stopping to pick up her own set of messages taken while she was out. Walking down the connecting corridor to her office, she barely glanced at them, nodding a greeting to those few employees left holding down the fort while the others were still out to lunch.

She closed the door behind her as she entered the small private office that had been part of the package of amenities that went along with her position as skip tracer. Wearily she plopped down into her cushioned swivel chair, punching the blinking button on her telephone to answer the call the operator had placed on hold as soon as she had seen her.

"Bobbi Morrow. May I help you?" Automatically

she pulled a note pad toward her and reached for a pencil.

"Yes, I think that would be highly desirable, considering that you have done everything in your power to do just the opposite." The deep masculine voice had a pleasing resonant quality that soothed, for the moment at least, Bobbi's perplexity over the caller's curious greeting.

Unconsciously her spine straightened just a bit and her fingers tightened around the pencil as she riposted crisply, "May I ask who's calling, please?"

"Of course. Blain Pearson. I'm sure you'll have no trouble recalling the name...you certainly didn't have any problem identifying my car, which for some ridiculous reason you had towed away yesterday, *Miss* — is it — Morrow?"

The straightened spine now assumed stiff proportions, and the pencil dropped onto the desk with a muffled clatter. Bobbi's jaw slackened for a moment as she sat stunned, truly taken off guard as she realized that the person to whom she was speaking was exactly who'd been nagging at her mind. She would have been surprised in any event, even if it had not been the professional athlete; as long as she had been employed in her present capacity she had not heard from a single person whose car she had managed to track down and have repossessed. Someone guilty of reneging on a loan financing contract was not likely to step forward and present his face to the world.

"Yes," she answered tentatively, warily cautious as she waited to hear just what the man had to say.

"How—how did you get my name?" she inserted on second thought.

The question elicited a half laugh, a gruff sound that suddenly brought to mind a picture of the man. Bobbi possessed a more than ample supply of photographs of Mr. Pearson in her file; all of them newspaper shots of the Washington Bullets player, each disturbingly revealing of a long, lanky body meagerly covered by the shiny, sweat-slickened fabric of a basketball jersey. Legs—long, hard, sinewy legs—suddenly flashed before Bobbi's eyes, and she felt her neck grow hot and clammy as an unpleasant flushing sensation began to build.

His reply was thick with sarcastic overtones. "Your storage lot in Sterling, which I *finally* happened to locate, was perfectly willing to reveal the name of the party responsible for having my car towed away. I don't know if that's the usual case, but I've never had the chance to find out before. This is a first for me."

Bobbi cleared her throat and retorted briskly, "Mr. Pearson, I would suggest you direct any questions you may have to the credit department. I was handling your case, but it's now out of my hands."

"I see," he answered dryly. "And whose hot little hands is my 'case' in now?"

"As I said, the credit department. You can talk with Mr. Charles Lambert. He's the supervisor."

"Am I correct in understanding that it was you, Miss Morrow, who actually saw to the impounding of my car?"

"That's right," said Bobbi tersely, her eyes narrowing suspiciously. What was this all about?

"Then it would seem to me that *you* are the person responsible for clearing up this ridiculous situation," he insisted.

"Mr. Pearson," Bobbi retorted rigidly, grasping for the upper hand in this increasingly disturbing conversation. "As I told you a moment ago, I am no longer handling your case. It has been turned over to the credit department, and if you have any further questions, I suggest you direct them there."

"I think it would behoove you, Miss Morrow," he suggested smoothly, "to get my case back into your eager hands. That is, if you wish to continue discussing this matter with me, instead of my attorney."

Bobbi was not one to take threats lightly, nor to overreact to them unnecessarily.

"It really makes no difference as far as I'm concerned, Mr. Pearson," she replied unconcernedly. "If you prefer to have your attorney handle the matter for you, I would be more than happy to speak with him."

"Mmm-mm. Then I assure you, Miss Morrow, you may have the opportunity to do just that very soon."

"Fine," Bobbi answered pertly. "Good-bye, Mr. Pearson."

Without waiting for any reply on his part, Bobbi hung up, somewhat startled to find that her hand, still clutching the receiver, was shaking visibly. For all her bravado she had to admit that Blain Pearson had done an excellent job of provoking a distinct attack of nervous tension.

Which was absolutely ridiculous, Bobbi chastised herself immediately. Why in the world should she respond to someone who was no more than an expert

con artist? He had conned AMAC into providing him
with a loan on a sports car obviously beyond his
means, and now he was trying to con her into thinking
that he was innocent of any wrongdoing. She shook
her head absently at the blatant arrogance the man
displayed so readily. What did he hope to accomplish
with such abrasive behavior? Most likely he had conjured up some phony story to excuse the fact that he
had not remitted one single payment on the loan he
had taken out over six months earlier. She had heard
of such ruses from skip tracers in other AMAC
branch offices, but as yet had not had any such en-
counters herself.

Whatever his ploy, Bobbi was certain it would be
cleverly convincing. Just speaking with Blain Pearson
was enough to reveal he was no fool. Forgetting about
the messages still awaiting her attention, Bobbi crossed
the room to her file cabinet and opened the drawer containing Blain Pearson's file.

Scanning through its contents, she walked back to
her desk, automatically reaching out to place her hand
on the back of her chair and turn it around before she
sat down in it. There was nothing amiss within the
pages of the rather thick folder. The most important
document, a copy of the loan contract, was there
amongst the abundant notices to Mr. Pearson, telling
him that his account was delinquent, all of them un-
answered. Bobbi slowly shook her head; whatever excuses he might use to defend himself would have to
be more than just a little clever. All the evidence she
needed to substantiate her actions in having traced his
whereabouts for the past six months and then arrang-

ing for the repossession of his Corvette was right there. She closed the folder, mentally soothed by the reassuring knowledge. Let Mr. Blain Pearson set his lawyer on her if he liked; she certainly stood on solid enough ground to face him.

Her absorption in the matter was so intense that Ralph abandoned his booming knocking on her door-jamb, walked directly into Bobbi's office, and took the only seat available, a straight-backed wicker chair across from her desk. She glanced up in surprise to see him sitting there, staring at her curiously. Blinking once, she said, "Oh, hi, Ralph." Two vertical lines creased the bridge of her nose, and a corner of her mouth lifted in a bemused grin.

"What's wrong? Do I look that bad?"

Ralph cast her a speculative glance. "You never look bad and you know it. No...I just consider it a little odd when you don't respond to ten or more knocks on your door."

Bobbi pushed herself out of the chair and walked back to the file cabinet, replacing the folder in its proper drawer. "My mind was a thousand miles away. I don't think I'd have heard a bomb if it went off in the hallway."

"Oh? What's up?" Ralph pushed up his glasses, a sure sign that his interest was piqued.

"Blain Pearson called," Bobbi stated, sliding the file drawer shut.

"You're kidding," Ralph commented, crossing one knee over the other and folding his arms over his vest-clad chest.

"I'm not," she assured him, returning to her desk and picking up the ignored pile of messages. "He's threatening to let his lawyer handle the matter of his repossessed car."

"Ha! That's a new one for you, isn't it?" Ralph raised both eyebrows.

"Yes, but nothing I can't handle," Bobbi stated firmly. "Whatever story Mr. Pearson has about his innocence in the matter will be easily squelched the minute his attorney takes a look at his file."

"Somehow I get the impression you're more upset about this call than you're letting on."

Bobbi winced. Sometimes it seemed as though Ralph could actually read her mind. But it was understandable, she reflected; after all, the two of them had known each other for as long as Bobbi had worked for AMAC, and their relationship extended beyond the boundaries of a working environment.

Sighing, Bobbi leaned forward, propping her elbows on the desk, linking her hands together palms down and resting her chin atop them. "All right," she admitted. "He did get to me. But it doesn't matter. It's all over with anyway. The situation is out of my hands. He'll have to go through the credit department if he has any further complaints."

"You told him that?"

"Of course. He didn't like it one bit either."

Ralph snorted knowingly. "No, I don't imagine he did. But I suppose he has every right not to. So"—he slapped both hands atop his thighs and stood up—"what have you got planned for this weekend?"

Bobbi groaned and leaned backward, tilting her

chair as she stretched her arms out in front of her.

"Nothing but chores that need to be taken care of. Washing, cleaning, more washing...pure drudgery."

"How would you like to interrupt that exciting agenda by taking in a movie with me tomorrow night?"

Bobbi smiled up at Ralph with a meaningful twinkle in her eyes. There were times when it was obvious that Ralph was ready for a deepening of their relationship, but Bobbi held back tenaciously. In spite of the fact that it would be so...*practical* to let it happen, she couldn't help the inexplicable reluctance she felt. She needed more time.

Ralph was well aware of her feelings and now, as always, was totally respectful of them. Immediately he qualified, "Just a movie. Really."

"All right, then," she agreed. "Why don't you give me a call tomorrow afternoon?"

Ralph grinned. "Sounds good. Talk to you then." Giving a brief nod in farewell, he left the office, enabling Bobbi to get back to work.

Bobbi often car-pooled with several other employees of AMAC's corporate office in Arlington, Virginia, having found it advantageous to share the costly expense of transportation with those living near her apartment in Maclean. By the time the six of them pushed their way through the traffic jams clogging the beltway and every other thoroughfare they were required to travel, the clock was edging toward seven o'clock.

Bobbi was glad she hadn't made plans for that evening. She was feeling the effects of the long, sleepless week and was looking forward to a simple evening alone; nothing more involved than preparing a light meal, turning on the television to the best of whatever mindless programs it had to offer, and curling up on the living room couch until she drifted off to sleep.

She set about doing just that as soon as she climbed the three flights of stairs to her apartment. First things first, she decided, shrugging out of her quilt-lined trench coat, simultaneously kicking off her shoes. She finished undressing in the bedroom, then donned her long comfortably warm wine-colored velour bathrobe and slipped into a pair of matching furry house slippers. As she made her way to the kitchen she glanced around appreciatively. She'd spent a small fortune on the room, decorating the mustard-yellow walls with a myriad selection of baskets interspersed with shiny copper kitchenware. Living alone was not as easy as she had anticipated, but having a homey, cheery place to come to every night definitely made the feat a good deal more bearable.

Considerably more relaxed then, she began preparing her supper by steaming artichokes, sautéing mushrooms, and warming the French bread that she had started on a couple of days earlier. She set it all on a tray and carried it into the living room, placing it atop the walnut-and-glass coffee table. Picking up the remote control device, she plopped down on the couch and switched on the television, digging into her meal eagerly, feeling the tautness of her neck and shoulder muscles begin to relax as her mind did.

She had just buttered and bitten into a piece of

crusty French bread when the doorbell rang. A trifle irritated with the untimely interruption, she pushed the sound button on the remote control to silence the set. Still chewing, she covered the distance from the living room to the small foyer quickly and unlocked the bottom lock of the door. Swallowing, she pulled the door back, leaving the chain in place and peeking through the crack to see who her unexpected visitor was.

Later Bobbi reflected that she'd been fortunate in having swallowed the bread mere seconds before her eyes took in the sight of the incredibly tall and lanky stranger standing just outside her door. If an antelope had been standing there, her eyes could not have bugged out more.

Impossible, she thought, gulping spasmodically. What in the world was Blain Pearson doing standing on her doorstep?

Chapter Two

Bobbi stared mutely, barely aware that her mouth was hanging agape. She wondered if perhaps she was witnessing an apparition of sorts. Not so, she discovered immediately as he spoke, obviously having waited long enough for a greeting from her, which was not forthcoming.

"I am looking for Bobbi Morrow," he said in the same rich, resonant tone she recalled from their telephone conversation that afternoon. He shifted his weight onto one foot as he spoke, the slight lowering of his incredible height doing nothing to ease the angle at which Bobbi was forced to raise her head to look up at him.

Bobbi's eyes narrowed warily as she studied the giant before her. Her gaze swept down the length of him, making a quick comparison of Blain Pearson in the flesh with Blain Pearson in the various photographs she'd kept in his file. Black-and-white photography had given the thick, well-cut hair a dark brown or black appearance, not revealing the deep red tint that cast it an auburn hue.

A healthily bronzed face and ocean-blue eyes added another dimension not depicted in the pictures. The lean, ruggedly hewn body that the beige wool slacks, dark brown shirt, and tweed sport jacket covered now was another matter altogether. Bobbi had seen enough of it to know there wasn't any improvement necessary in that department. Blain Pearson was a breathtakingly handsome man, in spite of his ridiculous height, and she really should stop dwelling on it and do something besides standing there and gawking at him like an idiot.

"I'm Bobbi Morrow," she answered as smoothly as possible. Her mind was racing in a whirl of conjecture. How had he found out where she lived? What was his real motive for showing up on her doorstep like this?

"Well, well," he murmured, his startling blue eyes peering at her through the sliver of space she maintained between door and wall. They seemed to glitter with amusement at the miniature figure standing guard behind the flimsy chain lock. Bobbi was suddenly aware that one hefty shove from one of those booted feet would be more than adequate to gain entrance to her apartment if he so desired. Instinctively her hold over the latch and doorknob tightened and she narrowed the gap even more.

"Blain Pearson," she stated flatly, then added bluntly, "what are you doing here?" Her green eyes held his gaze unwaveringly.

"Oh, I think a little chat is in order, don't you?" he answered, his lower jaw suddenly moving in a rhythmical side-to-side motion. Bobbi watched the strange movement of his square jaw with open curiosity. What in the world? . . . Tobacco! *Chewing* tobacco. She grimaced. The man's physical appeal suddenly plummeted. If there was one habit a man possessed that was sure to turn her off, it was chewing tobacco. She'd never bothered to analyze the reason for her aversion to it, knowing only that she simply despised the habit. I should have known, she mused wryly. The typical jock—in every sense of the term.

"As a matter of fact," Bobbi answered sarcastically, "'little chats' happen to bore me immensely. So if you don't mind..." Her voice trailed off meaningfully and she shifted her weight, a gesture reflecting that the unexpected interruption of her evening was wearing her patience thin.

Blain's rugged jaw worked again, then stopped. "Well," he drawled, "looks like you'll have to be bored for a while tonight, Miss Morrow." His gaze hardened, indicating that whatever patience she may be deficient in he possessed in abundance. "I thought, since you were so unwilling to discuss my plight over the telephone this afternoon, you might be more amenable to a personal visit."

Bobbi's patience was now on the verge of snapping; her expectations for a nice quiet evening alone were suddenly evaporating. If she was to salvage any of it, she'd have to get rid of this irritating, tobacco-chewing jock immediately.

"As you can see, Mr. Pearson," she answered tartly, "I'm not exactly dressed for a visit from anyone...let alone a stranger."

His bold blue eyes lowered their gaze from her face to follow the smooth ivory column of her throat, resting just above the hint of cleavage revealed by her loosening bathrobe. Bobbi felt a warm flush creep up the base of her neck and instinctively she reached for the lapels of the wine-colored material, fingers clutching it tightly against her throat.

"I hardly think I qualify as a total stranger." His rugged jawline rotated again and his eyes twinkled daringly. "I'm not too particular about clothes anyway."

The warm flush ignited to an angry spark, and Bobbi spat back, "Since you evidently didn't get the point earlier, I'm going to say this one more time, Mr. Pearson. If you have any further questions about your repossessed car, you will have to take it up with the credit department."

His dark brows shot up questioningly. "But I was told that *you,* Miss Morrow, are a member of that department."

"Technically, yes. However, the bulk of my job is simply to obtain information to enable me—the company, that is—to track down those individuals—and their automobiles—who have defaulted on their accounts."

"Such as mine?"

"Exactly."

"Ah, but you see, Miss Morrow, that is where you have made a serious mistake. I make good all my debts and I assure you I have not defaulted on anything with your company."

Bobbi opened her mouth to voice an objection, but Blain hastily interjected, "Tell me, have you spoken to anyone outside the credit department about this?"

"Why would I?" She frowned.

Blain reached inside the inner pocket of his jacket

and withdrew a long white envelope. He held it up for an instant, then slapped it against the palm of his other hand.

"Well, for instance, if you had checked with the title department, you might have discovered this."

The vertical furrow along the bridge of her nose deepened as Bobbi stared at the envelope. "What is it?"

The rotating motion of his jaw resumed for a few seconds, then stopped, the twinkle in his eyes fading as he stared down at her with a totally serious look.

"The title to my car."

"Wh-what do you mean?" she asked, perplexed.

"Just what I said. The title to my car, which, as a matter of fact, has been in my possession for the past several months."

Bobbi swallowed convulsively and her sea-green eyes widened in dismay. "But—but that couldn't be," she stammered.

"Oh, yes... it could," Blain asserted smoothly. He put the envelope back inside his jacket and placed both his hands on his hips. "Do you think I could come inside? It's getting rather chilly standing here."

Bobbi was all too aware of that fact; the nippy early spring evening was bringing goose bumps to her flesh as its cool breeze slithered up the long skirt of her robe. Her brain was rapidly ticking off the consequences to his unbelievable assertion. No doubt he was merely trying to pull the wool over her eyes. But then, if what he claimed had a shred of truth to it, she would do well to invite him in. Naturally his story was highly unlikely, but she may as well hear him out.

Besides, he was right about one thing—it wasn't as though she'd be letting in a total stranger.

"All right..." she answered, hesitating, then removing the latch and swinging the door open. "Come in. I— You can wait in the living room while I change."

Blain followed her inside the foyer, his enormous frame suddenly reducing the entire scale of the normal-size apartment. With a wave of her hand Bobbi offered him a chair, then hurried from the living room into the tiny hallway and to her bedroom, closing the door shut behind her. Hastily she slipped into a pair of faded snug-fitting jeans and pulled on a green woolen turtleneck sweater. She gave her rather tangled hair a brush-through and picked up a tube of lip gloss that lay on her dresser. Her hand stopped in midair. What was she doing? What difference did her appearance make? Certainly none to Blain Pearson. She need only listen to his improbable story and then get rid of him.

Blain sat down in the shiny vinyl swivel chair Bobbi had indicated. It was, he noticed, like the other contemporary furniture in the room; the sort to make a person feel comfortable enough to not want to get back up again. He glanced at the half-eaten meal on the coffee table and shook his head slowly. Women! Always on diets. Imagine filling up on that kind of rabbit food!

He crossed one leg over the other, propping an ankle across his knee. He smiled to himself, thinking how inaccurate his image of Bobbi Morrow had been. This tiny feminine creature certainly didn't jibe with the hefty, ferocious amazon he imagined he'd talked to over the phone earlier. Although it was all too clear this little pip-squeak was just as much in love with her own measure of power as any amazon, the execution of which had cost him a hell of a lot of trouble.

Blain's initial fear that his Corvette had been stolen had been rapidly transformed into cold fury upon discovering that it had actually been towed away... and under the orders of the finance company he'd paid off several months earlier. He'd received several notices during that time from the credit department that he was late in making payments, an obvious error on their part that he could ill afford the time to deal with. Nevertheless he had corresponded with the title department, asking that they straighten out the blunder. Having been assured by a representative that the matter would be taken care of, he had subsequently ignored the rest of the notices. He'd been on the road so much that he'd barely had time to keep up with his mail, let alone take care of such minor problems.

Minor had turned out to be a most inappropriate term, he'd discovered. After battling his way through the expected amount of red tape involved in finding out what in hell had happened to his car, Blain had finally learned the name of the person responsible for the ridiculous shenanigan. A woman's voice responding to the name Bobby had taken him aback at first, but his surprise had been swiftly overshadowed by her obvious disinterest in hearing his plight, apparently all too willing to send him right back into the web of red tape from which he had just emerged. Generally speaking, Blain Pearson had always considered himself a mild-mannered person, not one to waste precious mental energy on such useless emotions as anger or revenge. However, this case was definitely an exception to the rule. Something had snapped inside him when the insensitive broad had simply dismissed him, ordering him to take his problem elsewhere, totally unconcerned about the inconvenience her mistake had wreaked upon him.

One glance through the telephone pages had revealed what he wanted to know: her address. He'd have felt no compunction whatsoever at concocting some story to extract the information from the company's personnel department if he'd needed to. But such wasn't the case. The foolish woman listed her entire name in the telephone book. So much the easier for him.

The cab fare had been exorbitant, but he intended to charge every cent the inconvenience of not having his car created to AMAC, a fact that, in addition to the other interesting data he'd uncovered about Miss Morrow, would not look good on her record. But it would be well worth it, he'd mused quietly on the way over. He could inconvenience her just a little, too.

As he sat in her comfortable cleverly decorated apartment, taking in all the indications that she was there alone, Blain wondered at the reason for it. She was not an unattractive woman, he was thinking... surely she would have other plans for a Friday night than simply spending it alone. Bobbi walked into the room just then, and Blain hastily modified his estimation of her physical attributes. He had not missed the softly rounded curves the velour material clung to as she had left the room earlier, but the jeans and sweater she wore now almost parted his lips in an oath he hadn't even thought of in years. His taste in women ran toward tall, willowy types—a matter of practicality as much as anything else. Well, well, well, he thought to himself, dynamite sure as hell does come in small packages. *It sure as hell does,* Blain thought, swallowing deeply.

Bobbi had to steel herself against the awesome picture the handsome giant sitting in her living room presented. Even when he was seated, one couldn't help but be aware of his incredible height. He simply dominated the room and anyone else who happened to be around, which, at that moment, was her, she realized. Staunchly she entered the room and crossed to the coffee table, picking up the tray that held her now-cold supper and carrying it to the kitchen. This was her apartment, she reminded herself firmly. No stranger was going to usurp that plain fact by his mere presence. The thought, meant to be reassuring, was somehow an exceedingly weak one. The physical reality of the situation was that he was the larger of the species, and she, being the infinitely stupider, had allowed him free access to her home!

"I'm sorry I interrupted your supper," Blain apologized.

Bobbi shrugged, pulling out a drawer loudly and withdrawing a roll of aluminum foil with which to wrap the leftover food. Her appetite had vanished approximately fifteen minutes earlier—the moment she'd opened her door to see him standing there. The point now was to steer the conversation toward the subject of Blain Pearson's dubious assertion that he possessed title to his car.

"Doesn't matter," she dismissed lightly. She finished in the kitchen, then returned to stand just inside the doorway connecting the living area, leaning against the doorframe and crossing both arms over her chest. "Now, what is this about your claim to having clear title to the automobile we repossessed?" Precluding his answer, she raised one hand, palm outward, and cocked her head to the side.

"Believe me, Mr. Pearson, such a mistake is highly improbable, so whatever story you've concocted had better sound awfully convincing." Her sea-green eyes slanted in feigned tried patience, not unlike a mother hearing out a child's excuses for a bad report card. In actuality, however, she was growing increasingly tense from Blain Pearson's unnerving presence in her living room. Speaking to him over the telephone had been a great deal easier. With a sinking sensation in the pit of her stomach, Bobbi realized she'd made a serious mistake in not having heard him out then.

Blain stared at the petite, sensuously proportioned woman staring haughtily back at him with amusement and a measure of begrudging admiration. For her size she certainly wasn't lacking in spunk. As his jaw began to move again his eyebrows raised in surprise when he saw her grimace in distaste.

"Is something wrong?" he inquired. "Besides my presence, that is."

Squaring her shoulders, Bobbi moved into the room, sitting down on the edge of one corner of the couch.

"Actually," she stated, "I'm rather concerned about my apartment." She arced one arm in a demonstrative gesture. "As you can see, a spittoon is not part of my decor."

Blain's angular jaw ceased movement, and he almost choked.

"What is that supposed to mean?" he asked, his blue eyes widening innocently.

"It means," Bobbi answered pointedly, "that I'm not accustomed to having tobacco chewers in my home, so if you don't mind, I'd appreciate it if you'd take care not to soil any of my furnishings."

Blain stared at the completely serious expression on Bobbi's face for a mere second before exploding into a hearty belly laugh. Bobbi frowned her disapproval of his finding humor in the situation and then watched in astonishment as he rose from the chair and ambled through her living room to the kitchen with all the ease in the world; one would think he actually lived there! Blain was still shaking his head as his boots clamored heavily on the tiled kitchen floor. He reached for the end of a roll of paper towels suspended beneath one set of cupboards, placed the gum he'd been chewing inside its folds, then threw the towel in the wastebasket.

With both his arms extended in front of him, his hands pressed down on the counter as he faced the opening in the wall that separated the two rooms. Bobbi's irritation magnified as she noticed how completely relaxed, even natural, his appearance there seemed.

He'd removed his jacket, and the sight of those

broad shoulders, smoothly hugged and framed by his form-fitting knit shirt, did something to Bobbi's insides. Unconsciously she swallowed, unsuccessfully trying to avert her eyes. But the ropey biceps were too inviting a picture, and her gaze followed them downward, across the trim waist, then up along the rigid column of his neck and angular jaw, finally meeting his blue eyes, watching her with unconcealed amusement. Shoring up every vestige of self-control, she managed with an air of cool aplomb, "May I ask what's so funny?"

"You," Blain answered, studying her curiously, as if she were some strange species he'd never before encountered. "You really thought I was chewing tobacco?"

Frowning her displeasure, Bobbi nodded mutely.

Blain's features contorted in barely suppressed mirth. "Then you will be relieved to know your carpet and furnishings are in no danger. It was only chewing gum." He cocked an eyebrow and said, "However... there seems to be something a little strange here."

"Oh?" Bobbi asked in a peevishly low voice, feeling rather foolish at having provided him with something to laugh at her about. "And what is that?"

"It strikes me as rather odd that a person who can dine on rabbit food for supper has the nerve to criticize someone who likes to chew tobacco."

Bobbi's eyes narrowed at the jibe and she asked haughtily, "What is that supposed to mean... rabbit food?"

Blain pushed away from the counter top and strode back into the living room, resuming his seat in the vinyl chair. He brought one long leg up, crossing its ankle over the knee of the other. The cushions made a whooshing sound as he sunk down into them and Bobbi grimaced at the noise, hoping the material wasn't stretched out of form too badly.

"Only that anyone who makes a meal out of artichokes and mushrooms doesn't have any business objecting to someone else's habit of chewing tobacco."

"One can hardly compare the two," Bobbi shot back dryly. "Artichokes and mushrooms happen to be considered respectable, even gourmet, fare in some of the most renowned restaurants." Suddenly the inanity of their conversation struck her, and Bobbi snapped, "But this has nothing to do with your reason for being here. Why don't we get to the point?"

Blain nodded agreeably, but the amused sparkle hadn't left his eyes, Bobbi noticed. Nevertheless she had no intention of voicing her objection to it, instead focusing her efforts on getting the explanation still due her.

As Blain did so, giving a most precise account of his troubles with the finance company over the previous six months, she listened quietly, her anxiety expanding to downright trepidation. The cocksure manner in which he related the story had a ring of honesty she couldn't completely ignore. An uncomfortable twinge pinched her stomach as she suddenly remembered an incident she had long since dismissed... or thought she had. No, it couldn't be. She mentally assuaged her doubts. By damn, it better not be!

The last thing she needed was another ridiculous faux pas to mar her well-established record of credibility. Fortunately the previous party involved had not seen fit to create a ruckus over the matter. One glance at Blain Pearson's mulish countenance was evidence enough that in this instance she'd best tread the churned-up waters *very* carefully.

When she spoke it was in a much more subdued tone than she had formerly employed, her features softer, even sympathetic. "First of all, Mr. Pearson," she began, "if AMAC is responsible for causing you so much trouble, I am truly sorry. As for my part, I was merely following a request by the credit department to locate your whereabouts and see to the repossession of your car." She lifted a shoulder in a gesture of helplessness. "But there is really nothing I can do about it at the moment. Our offices are closed throughout the weekend, so the soonest I can look into the matter is Monday morning."

While Bobbi spoke Blain watched with interest as the stubborn expression left her delicately carved features, replaced by a tender one that seemed to set her face aglow. Something deep within him stirred at the pleasant change in her personality. Perhaps she did care about his predicament. Again he felt himself being drawn to this miniature creature perched opposite him, and he was aware of an almost overwhelming urge to reach out and pick her up. He could have managed it with one arm, she was so damn tiny.

Suddenly he knew that Monday was too long to wait to see her, even speak to her again. It occurred to him also that he was not without a powerful measure of influence at that point. The information he'd accidentally overheard at AMAC's offices concerning

Miss Morrow's "flawless" work record could come in handy, if he chose to utilize it. Not a bad idea, Blain thought, not at all. Uncrossing his legs, he sat forward, leaning his elbows atop his knees and linking his fingers together.

"Monday isn't going to do me any good," he said, employing a severe tone. "The problem you've created has affected my entire weekend. I'm still without transportation."

"I'm sure AMAC will reimburse you for a rental car," Bobbi suggested, taken aback by his snide expression, such an abrupt change from his earlier humorous approach.

"Why should I go to the trouble of dealing with a rental agency?" he countered. "I shouldn't have to put up with the hassle that that would involve."

Bobbi frowned in perplexity. "But I don't know what else I can tell you. There's really nothing else to do."

Blain lifted his elbows off his knees and sat back, his head turning slowly as he took a long, appreciative glance around the apartment. "Oh, I can think of an alternative," he mused quietly.

Something sharp pricked Bobbi's insides—a warning that the handsome man lounging in her living room chair was no stranger to cunning and revenge.

"What?" she inquired, not at all sure if she wanted to hear the answer.

His gaze swung slowly back to her and his blue eyes glinted as he stared, revealing, more than the quiet forcefulness in his tone, that his alternative went beyond just that; it was an indisputable decision.

"Since you are the one responsible for causing me such difficulties this weekend," Blain replied smoothly, lifting one shoulder expressively, as if Bobbi could have no possible argument to what he was saying, "then it seems you should be willing to make up for it personally."

"How?" Bobbi asked.

"How?" he echoed, his gaze traveling about her apartment before stopping to rest on her wary expression. "By putting me up for the weekend. Here."

Chapter Three

It was Bobbi's turn to cough and sputter. Surely she hadn't heard him quite right.

"Wha— I don't believe I heard you correctly," she faltered, her green orbs reflecting utter dismay.

"Oh, I'm sure you did," Blain assured her smoothly, his expression cool and smug.

"But— I would think you'd want to stay at your own place near here," Bobbi declared, her brain trying desperately to decipher whether or not it was his idea of a joke.

Blain raised an eyebrow, and Bobbi flinched as he gazed at her with wry amusement.

"You're up on just about everything, aren't you? I suppose you know the address of my town house, too?"

Bobbi tried to feign an innocent look but, realizing it was futile, lowered her eyes to study her hands, which were absently massaging the tops of her thighs. Yes, she was well aware of Blain Pearson's address in Fairfax. Well, so what? That was part of her job.

"I thought so," he said, then added, "The only

thing is, your place is a hell of a lot more convenient for me this weekend. Also, mine's being leased out at the moment.''

Bobbi frowned and replied exasperatedly, "This is ridiculous! Surely you have some place you stay when—''

"True," he interrupted smoothly. "Usually with my parents, or with the team in a hotel.''

"So then you have plenty of choices. I don't see what difference it—''

"The difference," Blain inserted, "is that I don't care to go to the trouble of driving out to Fairfax—in a cab, of course—when I can just as easily stay here.''

"Easy for you, sure!" Bobbi threw back at him. "What about the situation it places me in?''

Blain raised one eyebrow and said, "You didn't seem to care too much about my situation when you hauled off and confiscated my car. Or Mr. Jeremy Sandover's.''

Bobbi's mouth twitched obviously and she felt as though he'd punched her in the stomach. She opened her mouth to speak but could summon absolutely no words to her lips.

Blain smiled benignly, "Oh, yes, I know all about that little skeleton in your not-so-clean work record.''

Incredulity fought with downright puzzlement as Bobbi sputtered, "B-but how did—''

"How did I find out? Let's just say that's for me to know and for you to wonder about." Blain waved a hand in the air dismissively. "It's all academic now anyway. I'm sure you'd prefer to keep that juicy tidbit between the two of us, right?''

Bobbi glared at him venomously. How dare he threaten her like this! And what in the hell was she doing gaping like a fool!

"Miss Morrow," Blain continued before she could get a word out, "I mentioned that I would not be averse to making a complaint to your supervisor over this matter. However," he added, cocking one dark eyebrow, "if we can find a workable solution to the problem you have created for me, then I don't see any reason for my having to even mention it. You could clear up the details with AMAC Monday morning, we could pick up my car, and"—he snapped a finger conclusively—"no questions need ever be asked."

"In other words, Mr. Pearson," Bobbi said, her jade eyes darkening with resentment, "you are blackmailing me."

Blain spread both of his hands before him, palms up. "A rather poor choice of words, but..." His voice trailed off as he shrugged lightly.

A slow burning sensation began building inside Bobbi, her hands clutching automatically into tight fists in lieu of hurling some heavy object at the devilishly handsome face gazing smugly at her. How ruthless could a human being get! she thought, furious with him for forcing her into such a ridiculous situation. The man had played his hand perfectly; she'd much rather see the matter hushed up, a fact he was obviously gambling on. But why? she wondered in total bafflement. Surely the man had other women waiting to run at his mere beck and call. Why in the world would he want to force himself on her like this for an entire weekend? The question stymied her, but she didn't really have that much time to analyze it. She looked up to find him leveling an expectant gaze at her.

Bobbi glared back at him stonily. He may have her over a barrel on this one, but she'd be damned if he'd think she was even remotely willing.

"All right," she bit out the answer. Her eyes smoldered as she continued. "I'll go along with your absolutely preposterous game, Mr. Pearson...for now."

Blain smiled his pleasure at her agreement, obviously not in the least concerned by her lack of willingness; he felt sure that it was merely a matter of time, their having a chance to get to know one another.

Bobbi raised one eyebrow questioningly. "I was under the impression you were here for a game this weekend."

"I am," Blain replied, still grinning. "We're up against the Lakers this Sunday."

"At the Capital Centre?" Bobbi queried.

Blain nodded.

"Don't you have to practice, or something, before then?"

"Yes," Blain answered, chuckling at her choice of terminology. "We usually do 'something' before we play. Our workout's tomorrow afternoon, in fact."

"So...what do you plan to do about it?" Bobbi asked. Surely he would be too tied up with his team to stay around her every minute that weekend, which would make the situation infinitely more bearable.

"Do about what?"

"About tomorrow afternoon," she answered, her annoyance undisguised.

Blain shrugged lightly. "I have to be there, if that's what you're getting at. Why?"

"Well...how do you plan on getting there?" She could have bitten her tongue; of course there was only one answer to that.

"In your car," Blain answered, sounding surprised that she should have asked. He added, "I don't have to be there until two o'clock, so we don't have to leave until one thirty or so."

"We?" Bobbi inserted dubiously.

Blain blinked innocently. "Yes, we. How do you think I'm going to get there? You took my car away from me, remember?"

Bobbi sighed in exasperation, then stood up, too agitated to remain seated a moment longer. Shoving her hands into the back pockets of her jeans, she walked through the living room and into the kitchen. Opening a cupboard door, she withdrew a glass and opened the refrigerator door, pulled out the lone carton of milk, and poured herself a glassful. Desperately she hoped the liquid would have the desired effect of making her drowsy. Sleep was definitely not going to be an easy thing to come by that night. The thought caused her to almost gulp down the swallow she'd just taken. Where in the world was Blain planning on sleeping? He'd very casually assumed that her services, specifically in chauffeuring him around town, were all a part of the cozy little arrangement. Well, he had another think coming if he thought that included bedroom favors as well.

Hastily Bobbi finished the rest of her milk and

turned to run the glass under the faucet. As she did so she almost jumped, completely startled to see that Blain had followed her and was leaning his giant frame against the door, watching her movements with the patience of a tiger stalking his prey. Bobbi felt her breath catch in her throat, amazed at the strange stirrings deep within her that caused her eyes to misbehave ludicrously. They seemed to be riveted on Blain's wide, well-shaped mouth, rendering her completely oblivious to the brilliant blue scrutiny her own soft lips were under.

"I—" Bobbi began, her throat suddenly parched, in spite of the soothing milk, "I only have one bedroom, Mr. Pearson," she finished forcefully.

Her words broke the spell of his gaze, and he grinned gamely.

"*Mr. Pearson* sounds silly, don't you think?" he suggested. "I think we're acquainted well enough for a first-name basis, don't you?"

Bobbi nodded her reluctant agreement, then, gathering her composure, she mumbled, "All right."

"I'll sleep on the couch," Blain reassured her.

"But—" Bobbi said, glancing at him uncertainly, "I don't think it will be long enough for you."

"It won't be the first time my feet have hung off the end," Blain said matter-of-factly. "Do you have anything besides milk to drink?"

"Oh, I think so," Bobbi said. Apparently he had no intention of invading the domain of her bedroom. The knowledge was immensely relieving, and she turned to open the refrigerator door a great deal more willingly than she would have moments before. "Let's see...I have Coke and orange juice and...here, a couple of beers."

"A beer's fine." Blain accepted the bottle, twisted the cap off, and threw it in the garbage pail in one corner of the kitchen. Taking a swig, he walked back into the living room.

Bobbi frowned suddenly and asked, "What about your clothes? You didn't bring anything else with you."

Blain sat down on the couch and watched the soundless picture on the television for a moment. Turning, he cast her a wry expression. "That's another problem you've caused," he informed her bluntly. "My suitcase is in the back of the Corvette. I don't have anything else to wear except my workout and uniform gear, which is with the team manager until Monday morning."

Bobbi lowered her eyes guiltily. She really *had* inconvenienced him—in more ways than simply having his car towed away unnecessarily. She was mulling over a reply when Blain spoke again.

"But you don't have to worry about pajamas for me. I usually don't wear anything to bed."

Bobbi looked up in alarm, but he was merely teasing her, she discovered. However, teasing or not, he really didn't have anything to wear, and even if he was courteous enough not to parade around in the buff, she couldn't very well expect him to sleep in a pair of trousers and a sport jacket.

"Hmmm," she muttered to herself, leaving the kitchen and walking past a now-reclining Blain to her bedroom. Blain had settled himself as comfortably as possible onto the couch and was busy toying with the remote control, turning up the volume of the television, and flipping through the various channels. He appeared as content as a lazy, self-assured cat.

Bobbi returned from the bedroom and remained standing in the doorway until Blain pulled his eyes away from the movie that had caught his attention.

"What's that?" he asked, pressing a button to lower the volume.

Bobbi held out the wine-colored velour robe she'd had on earlier.

"I thought you might be able to squeeze into this," she suggested, "or at least throw it around your shoulders. It's not much, but...I'm sure you don't want to sleep in what you're wearing now."

Blain turned down the corners of his mouth in silent contemplation, then caught the garment as Bobbi tossed it to him.

"All right," he agreed, pulling the robe across his reclining form and returning his attention to the movie.

An image of what he would look like in her robe forced its way into Bobbi's mind, and she was hard put to suppress a look of amusement. Instead she said, "I'll be in the bathroom for a while. You can have it when I'm finished."

Blain nodded once, then turned to face her again, both eyebrows raised expectantly. "Then what?"

Bobbi, having turned to walk away, suddenly stopped in her tracks. "What do you mean, 'then what'?" She frowned.

"Are you going to watch television with me? There's supposed to be a good late movie on."

Bobbi hesitated, lifting one hand to draw back a silky curtain of cinnamon-colored hair that had swung across one cheek.

"No...I don't think so," she declined. "I really need my sleep. This week hasn't exactly been the greatest in that department."

Mercifully Blain didn't argue with her. He simply nodded his understanding and turned back to watch television.

Such a strange person, Bobbi thought, returning to her bedroom to gather items for her bath. Once in the bathroom, she forsook a long soak in the tub, which she had earlier planned on, for a hurried scrubbing and rinsing in the shower, making record time of her regular routine. There was certainly nothing routine about tonight, she mused wryly, slipping into her two-piece pajama set and matching robe, then quickly returning to her bedroom. Inside, she switched on the bedside table lamp and returned to the door to lock it. Blain had done absolutely nothing out of line so far, remaining respectfully gentlemanly, but still...one never knows, she thought cautiously.

Climbing under the covers, Bobbi picked up the book she usually read a few pages of before falling asleep. Determinedly she forced herself to read, even turning the pages several times. The words, though, merely rushed before her eyes, making absolutely no mental imprint. She was much too conscious of the movements and sounds coming from the other part of her apartment.

The television was silenced for a while, followed by the heavy thud of Blain's footsteps as he went into the bathroom. The shower ran for quite some time, but it probably did take one heck of a lot of water to wash a body that enormously long, Bobbi thought.

The television came back on several minutes later, the volume respectfully turned down to muted proportions. At least *that* was a considerate gesture on his part, she thought wryly. With a heavy sigh, Bobbi closed the book and placed it back on the table, switching out the light. Turning onto her side, she closed her eyes willfully, a useless attempt to summon sleep. The milk hadn't done its job that night, she thought woefully. Undoubtedly it would help if she could think about something other than the strange set of circumstances she had involved herself in. More to the point, she admitted, something other than the disturbingly handsome Blain Pearson, lying that very moment on the other side of the wall, making himself right at home on her couch.

Trying to picture him fully stretched out on it was impossible, and Bobbi found herself wondering just how in the world he was going to sleep. Surely he would be cramped, uncomfortable... *What am I doing?* she chastised herself. It was *his* idea to force himself on her for the weekend. If she had to suffer the consequences of his need for revenge by playing host to him during the weekend, then he'd have to put up with a few inconveniences himself!

Chapter Four

Uttering a muffled groan, Bobbi flipped over onto her stomach and reached out with one hand to pull the extra pillow over her head. What in the world was going on next door? The fuzzy thought intruded on her sleep-drugged brain. Her next-door neighbor, Freddie, must have his kids over for the weekend. Pulling the pillow down over her ears to block out the noise, Bobbi frowned, thinking how uncharacteristic it was of Freddie to let his children create so much disturbance that early on a Saturday morning. He was usually a most considerate neighbor....

Suddenly Bobbi's eyelids flew open, her hands jerking the pillow off the top of her head as she pushed herself up, her tangled hair falling across her face. It couldn't be Freddie's children.... He had told her on Thursday that he'd be out of town that weekend and had asked her to keep an eye on his apartment while he was away. In one clarifying flash it all came back to her... the rude noises were coming from none other than her own television set, switched on by none other than Blain Pearson.

"Oh, God," Bobbi mumbled aloud, wishing she could go back to sleep and that the situation would fade into a mere dream. She'd even settle for a nightmare. Swinging her legs over the side of the bed, she sat up, rubbing the inside corners of her eyes as her body gradually became accustomed to its unwelcome state of awakeness. Dropping her hands, her head snapped around to the closed door, and she frowned severely.

"What in the world is he listening to?" she said, sliding her feet into the slippers next to the bed, then shuffling over to the closet. Falsetto voices and canned laughter reverberated through the wall separating her room from the living room. Saturday morning cartoons, of all things, Bobbi thought derisively. But what else should she expect? She grimaced, rolling her eyes heavenward at the sardonic thought.

Grabbing a pair of jeans and an old pink velour pullover—her favorite—she threw them both over her arm and walked toward the locked door, hesitating for a moment before opening it. The bathroom was only two steps away once she opened the door, but she clutched the flimsy nylon neckline of her pajama top close about her throat. If perchance he was in the immediate vicinity, she was going to be prepared.

In one swift movement Bobbi yanked the door back, covering the distance to the bathroom in record time and peering around the open door to make sure it was unoccupied before she slipped inside. Rocky and Bullwinkle were blaring loudly from the television, the silly cartoon undoubtedly having captured the brilliant jock's attention. Safely inside the bathroom, Bobbi shook her head, sighing audibly as she locked the door and set about performing her morning ritual. Annoyed at having been awakened earlier than usual on a precious day off, she purposely took her time, postponing facing the man in her living room for as long as was possible.

In the process of screwing the cap back on a bottle of moisturizer, the bottle clanked onto the tile counter top as a sudden banging on the door erupted, causing Bobbi to jump.

"You up yet?" Blain called out, sounding as cheery as if he'd been up for hours.

"No, I'm still asleep," Bobbi retorted sarcastically, clutching the bottle with one trembling hand. "I always sleep in the bathroom."

"Well, as soon as you're out of there, I'd like to get in. If you don't mind," he added with peppy politeness.

"Of course," Bobbi replied in a sugary voice. As if he hadn't had all morning to take his turn. Whose place was it anyway? she thought angrily, slowing down her movements even more.

Entering the living room, Bobbi hesitated for a moment, watching with amazement as Blain sat with his back to her, his long legs stretched out across her sofa and hanging over the arm of the opposite end, her velour robe barely covering the tops of his knees. A sugar-coated cereal commercial was blaring its tempting message to millions of sugar-intoxicated juveniles, Blain Pearson's attentions as captivated as any five-year-old's. Noisy crunching sounds competed with the television commercial as his hand traveled steadily from cereal box to mouth. He'd obviously raided her pantry and discovered her secret craving for Froot Loops. Bobbi's generation had been lured also and, unfortunately, she had not yet managed to kick completely the high-carbohydrate junk-food habit herself.

Despite her frustration with the situation, Bobbi experienced a strange mixture of laughter and bemusement gurgling up in her throat at the scene in her living room. This really was for real! Hands on hips and shaking her head, Bobbi sighed heavily, the sound somehow penetrating Blain's preoccupation with the television screen. He turned to face her, a broad smile lighting up his face as his jaw chomped on the latest mouthful of cereal, his eyes scanning her in a lingering appreciative gaze.

Holding the box out and tilting it slightly, he produced a small frown as he swallowed. "This stuff tastes like vitamins. You eat this for breakfast every day?"

Her eyebrows dipped as Bobbi replied in monotone, "No. I don't eat it for breakfast." She paused, casting him a disparaging look. "And if you don't like it, why are you eating it?"

Moving about the living room, she straightened up the throw pillows on the love seat, and rearranged the various odds and ends on the low coffee table, ignoring as best she could the giant intruder sprawled across her couch.

"I'll eat anything when I'm hungry," Blain replied, fumbling inside the box for another handful, his gaze reverting to the antics of Bullwinkle and Rocky on the television set.

Shrewishly Bobbi reached out and turned down the volume. "Are you also hard of hearing?" she snapped, turning to intercept the indulging look Blain was giving her backside.

"I'm sorry. Was it too loud?" he asked innocently.

"Yes, it was." Bobbi glared at him for a moment, then strode out of the room and into the kitchen.

After downing a few more handfuls of the vitamin-enriched cereal, Blain watched as Bobbi opened the refrigerator door and poured herself a glass of grapefruit juice. "What's for breakfast?" he asked enthusiastically.

"What?" Bobbi gulped, setting the glass down on the counter with a thud, her expression indicating she couldn't have possibly have heard him right.

"We *are* having breakfast, aren't we? Most important meal of the day, you know. I myself can't get through the day—"

"I don't care *what* you can or can't do, Mr. Pearson," Bobbi retorted sharply. "For your information, this is not a hotel, or a restaurant, so if you want something to eat, you'll have to go out and get it yourself."

Blain lifted one shoulder and cocked his head. "Okay. But you'll have to take me. I don't have any transportation, remember?"

"Oh!" Bobbi exclaimed through her teeth. "Why did I ever agree to this ridiculous scheme?"

"You should have asked yourself a similar question when you had my car impounded."

Bobbi turned her back to him, opening the refrigerator door with such a vengeance that the bottles on the door shelves rattled. She wasn't going to dignify *that* with an answer, that was for sure. Counting to ten slowly, she turned back around, produced a plastic smile on her face, and said, "All right, Mr. Pearson—"

"Blain," he corrected, smiling his friendliest of smiles.

Bobbi rolled her eyes upward. "Whatever..." She dragged out the word. "What I was going to say— Blain—is that if you desire more of my food to eat, then you can fix it for yourself. I don't eat breakfast."

"You what?" he responded, dark eyebrows arching upward sharply.

"I don't eat breakfast," Bobbi repeated slowly, as if speaking to someone mentally deficient. Opening the door to the automatic dishwasher, she began emptying it of the cleaned contents.

Suddenly Blain appeared in the doorway of the kitchen, the top of his head almost touching the doorframe.

"But breakfast is the most important meal of the day," he insisted with all the fervor of a television evangelist delivering a Sunday morning sermon. "Your brain needs fuel the same as your body does... in the morning especially. It makes all the difference in the world as to how you feel and perform all day long."

Bobbi stood on tiptoes to place a stack of plates on the upper shelf of the cupboard next to the electric range.

"I feel fine in the morning," she answered. "I have enough 'fuel' of my own."

"Ah, but that's only what you think," Blain insisted, stepping into the kitchen and opening the refrigerator door, his eyes scanning the contents of the sparsely stocked interior. "Let's see...not much. Hmmm. Eggs—good. A little milk—that helps." Withdrawing both, he turned to her. "You do have bread, don't you?"

Bobbi clucked her tongue and sighed exasperatedly. "Yes, I have bread. In the pantry. Why—"

"Great," Blain said, moving past her and opening the pantry door, withdrawing the loaf of half-consumed bread and placing it on the counter next to the range, along with the eggs and milk.

"What do you think you're doing?" Bobbi asked, feeling distinctly shoved out of her own kitchen as Blain moved within its small confines, the Galloping Gourmet setting to work in earnest.

"I'm making breakfast for the both of us," he answered, rifling through cupboards and drawers, withdrawing an assortment of bowls and plates and utensils, and turning on one of the burners on the range. Looking at Bobbi, who now watched helplessly from the doorway, he cast her a toothsome grin and continued. "You scoot out of here for now. By the time you've had what I'm gonna whip up, I'll have you eating breakfast like a regular trooper."

Bobbi's mouth parted and remained open for a few seconds, the objection she was about to voice dying away in her throat as Blain set about the job of preparing whatever it was he thought she was going to eat.

Resignedly she turned and walked back into the living room to switch off the television set, clamming up

Fred Flintstone midsentence. Why? she berated herself inwardly. Why was she going through with this? How was she going to make it through the weekend with this man? He acted as if he owned the damn place—tenant included. But then, a calming inner voice reassured her, it was only for two days, and if she just remained calm and went along with him, it would be over with before she knew it. He had promised that her virtue would remain intact; at least she had no fear on that score....

Blain's whistling filled the sudden silence created as she turned off the television set, and shutting her eyes tightly for a moment, Bobbi heaved a heavy sigh, deciding to continue with her routine chores for a normal Saturday morning. The aromas wafting through the apartment were surprisingly pleasing, and, strangely, she began experiencing a few twinges of hunger. Trying unsuccessfully to ignore them, she set about straightening the bedroom and bathroom, piling her laundry into a plastic basket and securing it with a long bath towel tucked over and around each side.

"Come and get it," Blain called out as she set the basket beside the front door. Walking back into the living room, Bobbi stopped, staring at the spread laid out on the dining room table. Blain had slipped back into his discarded clothes, apparently while she was in the back of the apartment, and he had tied one of her aprons—the blue-and-white gingham one—around his waist, the hem of it reaching the tops of his thighs.

"Come on," he urged her, placing utensils atop some paper napkins he had located in the pantry.

"I'm not hungry," Bobbi lied. Actually as she moved slowly toward the table the sight and smell of the golden-brown French toast, scrambled eggs, and mugs of steaming coffee whetted her appetite as powerfully as any meal she could remember.

Blain strode toward her and gently took her by the arm, guiding her toward one of the place settings. "Yes, you are," he insisted firmly, placing large hands atop her shoulders and gently pressing until she reluctantly took her seat.

Snapping his fingers, Blain strode across the living room floor once more and turned on and adjusted the stereo dial to a country music station. Taking his seat directly across from Bobbi, he lifted his mug of steaming coffee and saluted her. "To Bobbi, my most gracious hostess."

Bobbi looked at the handsome face across the table smiling at her and, in spite of herself, grinned as she moved her head from side to side. The food did look good, and her growling stomach was rapidly establishing precedence over her fading resistance.

"I don't know about the 'gracious,' part but I suppose I should eat it, since it *is* my food you've taken the liberty to prepare."

Blain had forked an enormous piece of French toast into his mouth and closed his eyes dramatically as he chewed slowly and thoroughly. Bobbi stifled a laugh at the silly picture he made, and resignedly she tasted her own food. Not bad, she admitted, grudgingly acknowledging Blain's culinary talents, not bad at all.

Blain seemed pleased that she was making an effort to eat and apparently enjoying it at that. Indeed Bobbi found her frame of mind improving dramatically as she finished everything on her plate. She got up to pour them both some more coffee.

"How long have you lived here?" Blain asked, stirring sugar and powdered creamer into the black liquid.

"Since I graduated from college," Bobbi replied, sipping her own coffee.

"And when was that?"

Bobbi leveled him a stare over the rim of her mug. "Is that a roundabout way of asking my age?" she asked wryly.

Blain inclined his head and shrugged one shoulder.

"I'm twenty-six years old, I graduated three years ago from the University of Virginia and I majored in Business with a minor in English lit. I've worked for AMAC for the past year and a half. That's it." She stared guilelessly at him. "Not nearly as glamorous as your illustrious basketball career, I'll admit, but then, not all of us are cut out to lead famous lives."

Blain drained the rest of his coffee and set the mug down. "I couldn't agree with you more," he answered, and Bobbi was puzzled by the sardonic tone he employed.

"What does that mean?" she asked, standing and starting to clear the table.

Blain picked up his napkin and dabbed at his mouth, pushed his chair back, and leaned backward, lifting his arms over his head and stretching lazily. "Just what it sounded like," he said noncommittally. His gaze rested on the basket of laundry next to the front door. "What is that?" he asked.

"What is what?" Bobbi asked, following his gaze. "Oh, the wash. What about it?"

"What are you going to do with it?"

Bobbi scoffed, "What a ridiculous question. I'm going to wash it, silly."

"When?"

"As soon as I finish cleaning up the mess you made here."

Blain glanced at his watch and then back at Bobbi.

"I don't know if you'll have enough time," he said, rising and clearing the rest of the table, then joining her in the kitchen.

"I don't have any idea what you're talking about," Bobbi snapped. "I always do the wash on Saturday mornings, and today is not going to be an exception."

"Well, if it's not, then you better get started," he commented, snatching the dish towel she was holding from her hands. "We should be leaving in another couple of hours."

Bobbi placed a hand on one hip and clucked her tongue in annoyance. "I suppose you're going to hold me to it, then; driving you clear into Maryland to the Capital Centre."

Shoving his hands down into the back pockets of his pants, Blain drew his lips together as he nodded. "That's right. So come on, let's get going."

Bobbi frowned, her green eyes narrowing warily. "What do you mean 'let's'?" Her gaze followed him as he walked out of the kitchen and into the living room, striding purposefully toward the front door.

"Two can get the job done faster than one," he

replied, bending down and heaving the basket effort-
lessly onto one shoulder.

Bobbi rolled her eyes helplessly, but she doubted it
would do any good to object. And besides, she really
did get tired of lugging the burdensome basket down
three flights of stairs and through the maze of sidewalks to the laundry room. If he wanted to relieve her
of the duty, she may as well take advantage of the
service.

"Which way?" Blain asked, stepping outside onto
the landing.

"Just a minute. I forgot the coins." Bobbi returned
to the kitchen, located the jar of coins she kept especially for doing laundry, and then joined Blain on the
balcony. "The laundry room for this section is down
that way," she pointed, starting down the steps ahead
of him, "but it's usually too crowded. So I walk over
to section C. It's more trouble to get there and back,
but at least you don't have to wait an hour for a machine."

Blain's longer stride caught up with Bobbi's shorter
one easily, and as they strolled down the sidewalks
connecting the brick three-storied buildings of the
complex, his head moved slowly from side to side as
he surveyed the surroundings.

"Nice place. I didn't notice that much last night,
but it really has a lot of charm."

"I like it," Bobbi responded to the complimentary
remark. "Especially the landscaping. Really lends it a
sense of privacy."

Section C laundry room was doing its usual amount
of Saturday morning business, Bobbi noticed immedi-

ately, but fortunately a few machines were available.

"You can put it down right here," she indicated, opening the lids on two of the washers and placing the required amount of change in the metal slots.

To Bobbi's complete surprise Blain set the basket down where she'd indicated, then pulled off the towel covering the rest of the bundle. He began sorting through the contents, chucking several items into the washer Bobbi stood in front of, reserving the rest for the one he faced.

"Darks in yours and whites in mine, all right?" he said as casually as if washing clothes with her were routine.

Bobbi's eyes widened disbelievingly, and a feeling of warmth began spreading across her face as she observed her more intimate undergarments being tossed by Blain Pearson's large, capable hands into the washer. Watching from the corner of her eye, she fumbled among her own pile of laundry, her mouth twitching nervously. She dropped a towel, bent to pick it up, and when she straightened, felt her face flush furiously as she observed Blain holding one of her bras, turning it this way and that, his head tilted back as he stared at it curiously.

Bobbi glanced over each shoulder and thanked God they were alone. Suddenly she reached out and snatched the garment away from him. "Give me that, would you!" she hissed.

"Tsk, tsk. What are you so excited about?" Blain asked in an infuriatingly lazy drawl.

"I'd appreciate it if you'd refrain from displaying my brassieres in public."

Blain's eyebrows rose and he nodded slowly. "Oh . . . so that's what it is; a bra."

Bobbi's face contorted into an expression of disgust and she placed a fist on one hip as she shot back, "Get out of here, Blain Pearson. I'm sure you've seen a ton of brassieres in your lifetime."

Blain inclined his head to one side and said, "I ain't never seen one as weird as that, lady."

Bobbi held the item in question up in front of her and said, "This is *not* weird. It happens to fasten in the front . . . not the back."

Blain studied the garment for a second, then nodded in appreciation. "Yeah. Not a bad idea." His blue eyes twinkled lecherously as they brazenly roamed Bobbi's chest. "Not bad at all."

"Oh!" was all she could exclaim, then she threw the bra into Blain's machine. "Just get on with it, would you?"

Not bothering to repress a snicker, Blain said, "Sure thing." The remainder of the task was carried out in silence, interrupted only once when he lifted the measuring scoop out of the detergent box that had been packed along with the laundry.

"How much?" he asked, poising the opened end of the box next to the small metal cup.

"Two," she answered curtly.

"Ready?" Blain asked, snatching up the basket and holding out his hand for the box of detergent as soon as she had measured out the proper amount for her machine.

"Yes," Bobbi answered, closing the lids and pulling out the dials, listening for the sound of water running into the machines to make sure they were working properly.

"Are you always this domestic?" she asked as they started back toward Section A.

He glanced down at her, raising both eyebrows questioningly. "What? Is knowing how to wash clothes the definition of domestic?"

"You also cooked breakfast," Bobbi reminded him.

"So?"

Bobbi shrugged. "I don't know. I just—it's just hard to picture a pro athlete doing those types of things."

Blain laughed at the sort of mental image she must have of him. "I'm not married, you know. And I don't have a full-time maid following me around the country, picking up after me and cooking all my meals. I *have* learned a few of the rudimentary lessons of living alone, you know."

"Aha! I knew it. A chauvinist at heart."

Blain broke stride for a moment, objecting. "Now, how did you get that impression of a nice guy like me?"

"From what you just said. You're not married, therefore you have to perform such mundane chores yourself. Therefore, if you had a wife, *she* would perform all the, quote, 'rudimentary,' lesser chores for you."

"Aren't those the usual duties of a wife?" Blain asked, employing an innocent tone.

"No! They're not. At least not in this day and age. I should have known...." Bobbi shot him a withering look, only to have it evaporate in the light of the teasing gleam in the azure eyes twinkling down at her.

"You should have known what?" he asked, one corner of his lips lifting upward in an amused grin.

"Oh, forget it," Bobbi answered disgustedly, irritated with herself for being baited so easily.

Gratefully she started the climb up the stairway to her apartment, glad for the opportunity to turn her back to the exasperating man.

"Don't you have any elevators around here?" Blain asked, shuffling up the steps behind her.

"Yes, but they're ridiculously slow," Bobbi answered, adding sarcastically, "I would have thought that you—being such a health nut and all—would recommend the exercise."

"Oh, I'm not objecting. I just thought it must be tiresome for someone with such tiny legs."

Bobbi had reached the third landing and she whirled around to face him. "Believe it or not, Mr. Jolly Green Giant, we shorties go through life quite contented with our stature. In fact, it's even desirable in many respects."

"Such as?" he inquired in that infuriatingly innocent tone, leaning against the wall as she fumbled with the key in the door.

She was just about to reply that she never had to worry about banging her head on the doorframe when entering a room when the telephone began ringing in the living room. Pushing open the door, she hurried inside and started for the telephone but dropped her keys and had to stoop to pick them up.

Blain strode in behind her and directly over to the telephone, picking it up on the fifth ring.

"Hello?" he answered, setting the basket down on

the floor and plopping down into the vinyl swivel chair. Bobbi stared at him in amazement. What incredible gall! she railed inwardly.

"Yes, here she is. Just a moment."

Guilelessly he smiled at her, reaching for the remote control device as she jerked the receiver out of his hand, glaring spitefully at him.

"Hello?"

"Bobbi? I thought I had the wrong number at first."

Bobbi winced. Ralph... Good Lord, she'd forgotten all about the plans they'd made yesterday. "Hi, Ralph," she greeted him in a careful tone.

"Who was that? If you don't mind my asking." She could almost hear the hurt in Ralph's carefully polite tone.

Bobbi sighed, moving as far away from Blain as the cord allowed. "Ralph, listen, you wouldn't believe me if I told you. It's... too involved. But we'll have lunch Monday, and I'll tell you all about it."

"What about tonight?"

"Ummm," Bobbi groaned, stalling. Swallowing, she answered, "I'm sorry. I can't make it. It—it's really complicated, Ralph. Believe me, if I could, I would, but—well—I'll just have to explain everything to you on Monday."

Silence. "All right, then," he said finally, quietly. "Doesn't sound like there's anything I can do to change your mind."

"Unfortunately, no." Bobbi's lids narrowed as she continued to glare at Blain, who had switched on only the picture on the television and was apparently engrossed in a soundless Japanese science-fiction movie.

"See you Monday, then," Ralph said disappointedly.

"Right."

Click. Bobbi replaced the receiver, placing both hands on her hips as she contemplated the consequences of her agreement to Mr. Pearson's demands. Breaking dates was inconsiderate and rude in her opinion, especially with people she really cared about. Hopefully Ralph would be his usual understanding self when she explained the circumstances.

It better be worth it, Bobbi seethed, chewing one corner of her mouth as she studied the back of Blain's well-shaped head for an instant, then turned on her heels and stalked out of the room.

Chapter Five

Bobbi lay down the copy of a romance she'd stashed inside her purse for what was bound to be an incredibly boring afternoon. Annoyed by her flagging interest in the rather predictable plot, she turned her head, letting her gaze take in the span of empty bleacher seats around her, trying her best to ignore the maze of activity going on on the court below, about none of which she had the least inkling of knowledge.

Nevertheless she couldn't help but eventually let her attention be captured by the practice session. It was incredible; she'd never seen anything like it. A few minutes earlier she had watched as a tall prematurely gray-haired man holding a clipboard, to which he gesticulated quite frequently, commanded the attention of the eleven giants surrounding him. Of course, she couldn't hear a word he was saying, but she understood completely as he shoved the clipboard beneath his arm and gave a single resounding clap.

All at once the place was filled with a cacophony of shouts and yells, rubber soles squeaking and slamming across the polished wooden floor as the practice began in earnest. Bobbi was absolutely amazed; there had to be twenty balls flying through the air, all aimed at the same basket! How in the world did they keep from colliding in midair? she wondered. Bobbi shifted in her seat and brought the book up in front of her. Her eyes followed the pattern of words, yet her mind would hear none of them. Slowly the book was lowered once again, and then her gaze singled out a particular player among the whirling, dashing bunch of them.

Auburn hair flying haphazardly around his well-shaped head, Blain's figure was without question the most riveting. Though he was not as tall as some of his teammates, there was something about him that would have made him stand out among any group of men. The natural lankiness of one so tall was balanced by a more than adequate physique. In fascination, Bobbi watched the straining, twisting, and flexing muscles. Sinewy arms were everywhere at once, glistening with the shine of sweat that also darkened the skimpy tank top and shorts. Rock-hard, hair-roughened thighs bulged and contracted in wondrous, ever-increasing motion.

Bobbi swallowed spasmodically as an image, totally unbidden and certainly unwelcome, made its way onto the screen of her mind's eye: her own diminutive body pressed against the granite hardness of him, squirming against—or with—the arms that bound—

Ridiculous! Bobbi chided herself instantly, slumping down in her seat. She picked up the novel once more and shoved it in front of her face, determined to put the damn thing to use. After several minutes of trying, Bobbi sighed in vexation and placed the book back in her purse and stood. It was no use; she had to do something besides just sit there. Oh, why did he have to insist on her taking him there! If only there was some place nearby she could have visited—shopping, anything—instead of leaving her stranded here in this ridiculously boring setting.

Thinking that it would be a hell of a lot better if her friend Mary Beth didn't find out about this one, Bobbi made her way carefully down the aisle; she was thirsty, and now was as good a time as any to search for a vending machine. Blain glanced up from the court just then and suddenly gave a wave and a wink. Bobbi could feel a slight burning sensation inching its way up the back of her neck as a series of whistles and comments immediately followed the obvious gesture.

Hurrying down the steps to the outer corridor, Bobbi fumed inwardly at the embarrassing scene. Embarrassing, of course, only for her. She had no doubt whatsoever that Blain's teammates simply assumed she was his local girl friend...or *groupie* would perhaps be a more apt term. Well, they could think what they liked. What difference did it make to her?

Slowly letting off steam, she walked up and down the east wing of the enormous Capital Centre, finding temporary amusement in the variety of activity going on there in preparation for the following day's game: workmen cursing vociferously above their hammering, the high-pitched whine of their power tools, squeaky wheels of supply carts rolling down the concrete aisles; all competing with the staccato dribbling of balls inside on the court.

Locating a soft-drink machine, she bought a can of cola and sipped at it absently as she returned slowly to the bleachers. A paltry grin lit her face as her thoughts returned to what Mary Beth would have to say about all this. Putting up a professional basketball player in one's apartment was an odd enough circumstance for anyone; for Bobbi it was absolutely unimaginable!

By the time she reached the stands again and reluctantly took a seat, Bobbi noticed that a lot more was happening down on the court than had been going on when she left. A group of scantily clad young women had assembled on the near side of the court and were talking and giggling as one of them began rigging up a record player. Soon they began walking out further onto the floor, positioning themselves into a prearranged pattern.

It was obvious from the diminished shouts and bouncing balls that not all of the players were focusing their attention on the practice session. The record player began grinding out some inane disco beat, and as Bobbi sat wryly observing them she rolled her eyes heavenward as the group of women—girls, actually, she amended as she got a closer look—began some sort of gyrating and twisting and kicking routine. Bumps and grinds would be a more apropos term, Bobbi thought derisively as she observed how very, very little material was wasted in designing those ridiculously short, revealing outfits they were wearing.

Who were they associated with, she wondered? Well, it didn't matter; undoubtedly they were the following day's entertainment, if one chose to term it such, which was exactly the reason she didn't have time for a sport such as basketball. Getting all dressed up to sit and watch a game that was poorly understood at best, then to have to sit meekly by and observe one's date salivating over all that bumping and grinding wasn't exactly Bobbi's cup of tea. What the hell was wrong with having a bunch of good-looking guys out there, strutting their stuff for the women in the crowd?

Bobbi's vexation was exacerbated a few minutes later as she heard the coach blow his whistle, then watched as the players called it quits for a while. Most filed off the court by way of the tittering, obsequious dancers, who by then were letting it all hang loose, reveling in the masculine attention they were receiving. Good God, Bobbi observed disgustedly, what more could they do except begin a striptease on the spot!

Most of the guys were drinking the canned fluid replenisher provided by the team trainer, and after a few minutes the music stopped, and the group of girls gathered around their own table. One particularly suave player swaggered on over, and pretty soon there was a general mingling among players and girls alike. Bobbi caught a glimpse of Blain, who was busy downing his drink; within seconds he too was caught up in the cozy scene as a buxom brunette sashayed up to him, all big eyes and smiles and thrusting chest.

Bobbi swallowed a bilious reaction to the gushy scene. She turned in her seat, even reached for the novel again, but her eyes returned quickly to the work-over Blain was getting from the ridiculous pushy broad. Her mouth twitched as a thought occurred to her: perhaps she wasn't being so pushy. Perhaps Blain already knew her. Bobbi gave a dry, quiet chuckle. Of course, stupid. Of course he knew her, just as he probably knew scores of others like her. Groupies, she thought disgustedly. She could summon nothing but utter distaste for the type.

Blain happened to glance up just then, and he caught her eye just before she purposefully lifted the book to her face. She'd be damned if he'd see any reaction at all from her, Bobbi thought nastily.

Mercifully the practice session ended much sooner than Bobbi had anticipated. After signaling that she would meet Blain back outside, Bobbi gratefully left the bleachers, relieved beyond words that it was over.

As they walked toward her Toyota across the parking lot Bobbi couldn't help but notice that Blain had obviously showered. She could smell the clean, fresh scent of him, and his wet hair, slick and shiny and plastered back from his forehead, took on a jet-black sheen, the auburn highlights giving way to those of midnight-blue.

"Hey, would you like me to drive?" Blain asked cheerfully.

"Sure, why not?" She shrugged unconcernedly. Actually he couldn't have made a better suggestion. She enjoyed it when someone else did the driving. A large chunk of her life was spent behind the wheel of a car, and any reprieve was more than welcome as far as Bobbi was concerned.

Blain had to shift the driver's seat back to its last position, but even then his legs were cramped in the small space. As he maneuvered the car through the acres of empty parking spaces he asked cheerfully, "Well, how'd you like it?"

"Like what?"

Blain slanted her a glance. "The practice session, that's what."

"Oh"—Bobbi nodded slowly—"that." She shrugged in feigned indifference. "It was okay, I guess. I didn't understand much of it."

"Like what?"

"Well...it was obvious you were all practicing some sort of plays. Is that what you call them?"

Blain nodded.

"Well, anyway, I was wondering why you never made any attempts to shoot for the basket."

"That's not my job."

"Why not?"

"Because my position is point guard, not scoring guard, who happens to score quite a lot in the game. A guard is mainly concerned with setting up plays and moving the ball down the court."

Bobbi nodded and gazed out the window. "Have you ever been hurt?"

Blain chuckled. "Sure. That happens to everyone. Why?"

"Because it just looked so, I don't know, so potentially dangerous out there."

"*Dangerous?* I must admit I've never heard that term used to describe basketball."

Bobbi turned her head sharply, her cinnamon-colored hair swinging about one cheek. "Well, it sure looked that way to me. All you guys out there dodging

each other left and right, balls flying helter-skelter...
It's a miracle no one gets smashed in the process."

Blain glanced quickly into both the side- and rear-
view mirrors, accelerating as he entered the interstate
loop.

"It's all in the timing," he explained. "Coordination and timing. That, and skill, is the name of the
game."

"Oh," Bobbi commented dully, leaning over to
switch on the radio, then staring back out the window.

"What's with you?" Blain asked in his never-
changing amicable tone. "Surely coming with me
wasn't that hard on you."

Shifting as she crossed her arms over her chest,
Bobbi answered, "No, not hard. Just boring as all
hell."

"Tsk, tsk. Aren't we touchy today."

Bobbi cocked an eyebrow and said sweetly, "And
I'm sure you can't imagine why." Sighing, she turned
to focus on the scenery flying past the window. "Anyway, it wasn't completely boring. In fact, I got a real
thrill out of watching Miss Boopsy Poopsy and the rest
of her troupe."

Blain made a half snorting sound through his nose.
"Wha— Miss who?"

Waving a hand in the air, Bobbi said disparagingly,
"Miss whatever. One of those half-naked chicks who
was salivating all over you."

Blain glanced at Bobbi out of the corner of his eye
and tried to keep the smile off his face. "I take it you
don't go for the halftime entertainment."

"Let me ask you this: Would you go for watching a

bunch of guys wiggling their rears while you're trying to watch a game?''

Blain inclined his head to one side and smiled then. "Let's hope I never do."

"So. I'm not in the least interested in watching a bunch of Vegas castoffs either. In fact, it bores the life out of me."

Such a hellcat, Blain thought to himself, grinning inwardly. No doubt she thinks I bed down with every last one of them. Smoothly switching the subject, he said, "Listen, you don't have any other plans for the rest of the afternoon, do you?"

It was Bobbi's turn to utter a half laugh. "Mmmm. I'm impressed. Expressing concern over *my* plans. How nice of you, Blain."

Blain sighed and blinked slowly. "All right. Cool it for now, okay? What I wanted to know is, do you have any objections to stopping at Tyson's Mall? I could use a few new things to wear."

He glanced dubiously at the slacks he was wearing, and Bobbi let her gaze follow to rest for an instant on his taut thighs; something a shade less snug would certainly be welcome as far as she was concerned. Quickly she averted her eyes to stare back out the window.

"All right," she agreed quietly. It'd been quite a while since she'd gone on a Saturday shopping spree; normally she avoided the stores like the plague because of the inevitable crowds. But today was different; she could use a little distracting noise and shoving.

And it was no wonder, the ironic thought hit her;

after all, look what she was having to tolerate for the entire weekend! A shopping spree, with crowds or not, would be a piece of cake.

The parking lots were jam-packed, and Blain had to slow the Toyota to a crawl as they circled and circled, finally lucking into a space within reasonable walking distance to the mall. Inside, the scene was much the same as outside. Throngs of people were drifting about the huge conglomeration of stores, reminding Bobbi of schools of fishes, swimming their strange, unpredictable patterns.

The seductive aromas of various foods assaulted them at once, reminding Bobbi of how long it had been since she'd eaten Blain's breakfast.

As if on cue, Blain asked, "Hungry?"

Bobbi nodded and answered, "Uh-huh. I—" Her gaze shifted suddenly to her left shoulder, where his large hand now rested comfortably, almost proprietarily. She frowned but oddly found it difficult to summon a protest of any sort. Her mouth parted as if to at least make an attempt, but Blain interrupted before one came to mind.

"How about a snack for now? I thought we'd have supper tonight at a favorite restaurant of mine I think you'll like. Reservations are usually required well in advance, but a good friend of mine manages the place, so that won't be a problem."

"You certainly have everything figured out, don't you?" Bobbi glanced up and cast him a calculating look. Her neck was gradually growing used to the strain of constantly arching backward to look up at him, but only then was she beginning to realize the impression the difference in their heights was making on certain passing strangers. More than one of the stares they'd received thus far had held a glimmer of disapproval; as if there had to be something immoral, if not downright illegal, in the two of them parading around in public like that. A sheer rebellious instinct seized Bobbi just then, and it was all she could do to keep from stepping closer to him. However, she was not about to risk any mistaken interpretation on Blain's part; meanwhile she determinedly ignored the curious attention they were receiving.

"I just happen to know you'll probably enjoy the place," Blain was saying, stopping outside the window of a men's clothing store that specialized in tall sizes.

"How about getting something to munch on, then we'll come back here," he suggested.

Bobbi agreed quickly, but the suggestion was put on hold as Blain's attention was suddenly diverted. A small group of teenage boys, having emerged from the crowd at some point, blocked their path as they started to walk away. One of them spoke up loudly as they all stared up at the tall man in open admiration. "Hey, aren't you Blain Pearson from the Bullets?"

Blain nodded and smiled. "That's what they tell me."

The jeans-and-T-shirt-clad group nodded and shifted in like fashion. "Hey, that's cool, man," the spokesman said. "Hey, Miko, c'mere." A short quiet fellow stepped forward and, at his buddy's request, turned to present his back. "Miko here is our walkin' autograph book. Would you mind addin' yours, Mr. Pearson?"

Blain chuckled, then accepted a pen from one of them as the group gathered around and watched as he penned his name to the boy's shirt. Bobbi was quickly lost in the shuffle as other admiring fans began to add themselves to the mini crowd surrounding Blain.

More than a bit perturbed by the whole scene, she wandered off from the lot of them and began to peruse the displayed items of a jewelry kiosk. Several minutes later she felt a hand on her elbow. She looked up to see Blain smiling ruefully down at her. "Sorry about that. Let's get out of here and get that snack."

They were lost in the mall crowd again, this time fortunately retaining the privacy of anonymity.

"Does that happen very often?" Bobbi asked as they strolled down another wing of the mall, sipping Cokes and sharing an enormous box of popcorn.

Blain shrugged and swallowed another handful of popcorn. "Mostly around here. Hometown athlete makes big and all that."

"Hmmm." They chatted for a while longer, and Bobbi could only surmise that Blain was quite adjusted to the loss of privacy in public. Well, it might be fine and dandy for him, she mused, but she could live far better without all the attention—none of which *she* received anyway.

Later she was hard put to keep the smile of amusement off her face as Blain tried on clothes in the tall man's shop. Maintaining a discreet distance from Blain and the salesman assisting him, she watched as he emerged from the dressing room to view himself in the three-way mirror; turning this way and that, glancing over his shoulders to observe the different views the mirror provided of his profile and backside, checking every angle, giving utmost attention to the way the material molded against his crotch and backside. Much to her surprise she was enjoying immensely the voyeuristic treat. He was an incredibly well-built man, she decided once again; every inch the lean, well-honed athlete. His height did wonders to the clothes he was trying on; shirts, jackets, pants... all of them hugged his figure perfectly, the material stretched to its fullest advantage and most alluring potential.

Bobbi began to feel almost lecherous, secretly ogling him that way. Embarrassed and more than a little perturbed by the recognizable gut reaction she was experiencing, she put a significant distance between herself and Blain until the fitting session was over.

Half an hour later the two of them were settled in the Toyota once again, slowly threading their way through the waiting lines of vehicles exiting the shopping mall parking lots.

"Sorry to put you through all that," Blain apologized as he inched the Toyota along.

Bobbi shrugged nonchalantly. "No problem."

"Good." Smiling, he slanted a glance at her. "Think you could stand another stop before we head back to your apartment?"

"Depends on what sort of stop it is," Bobbi answered, eyeing him warily.

"I usually try to check on things at the town house while I'm in town. We're not that far, so if you don't mind..."

Bobbi grinned ruefully and said flippantly, "My objections haven't made any difference so far...and, anyway, you're the driver."

Later she was to wonder why she hadn't gotten out of the car at that point and switched seats with him. The side trip to his town house was certainly not what she needed to wind up the day. The man's life-style was unreal! He was *most* definitely not her type.

"Who are you leasing it to?" she asked as they drove into the complex of three-storied contemporary town houses.

"Just some friends," Blain answered nonchalantly.

Some friends! Bobbi thought derisively as she fairly gaped in astonishment at the creature greeting them at the front door. If they made bikinis any briefer, Bobbi had neither seen nor heard of them. Indeed she wondered if *bikini* was even an appropriate term.

"Blain! When did you get in? Why didn't you call?" the blond very well-proportioned young woman gushed nauseatingly, and Bobbi's smile was perfectly plastic as she received a minuscule one from her.

"Marielle, I'd like you to meet Bobbi," Blain said as they walked on into the foyer.

Plastic smiles were exchanged again, and Bobbi was surprised to see that the blonde condescended to actually nod at her. That was the extent of her interest in Blain's companion, however, and for the next half hour Bobbi stood or sat in bored silence as Marielle and Blain discussed a variety of subjects, none of which had a thing to do with the town house itself. Check up on things. Bobbi winced inwardly. Ha!

Checking up on the nice dish he had stashed away in Fairfax.

By the time Blain indicated that he was ready to leave, Bobbi was about ready to jump out of her skin. Just why this brute of an intruder was working her into such an emotional uproar she had no idea. Nor did she deign to spend the time analyzing the fact.

"So," Bobbi said as Blain slid inside the driver's side of the car and started up the engine, "does that about take care of your agenda for the day?"

Blain raised his eyebrows at her tone and decided to play it safe for the moment. "Yes, it does. You didn't mind too much coming here, did you?"

Bobbi's eyes widened innocently. "Why, no, of course not."

Blain smiled, and Bobbi's eyes narrowed resentfully at the even handsomer picture he made with those white, perfectly even teeth. Turning her head sharply, she determinedly focused her attention on the pavement.

"Good." Checking his watch, Blain said, "We still have plenty of time to get home and get ready for supper. I could use a good meal by now."

Bobbi's growling stomach heartily agreed. Her brain, however, was another matter entirely. After spending the whole day with him, she wondered how in the world she could hold up for the rest of the night with the man.

Chapter Six

"You know," Bobbi said as she opened the door to her apartment, "I'm curious. You haven't mentioned your family at all."

Following her inside, Blain went on into the kitchen, opened the refrigerator door, and extracted the last beer.

"What about 'em?" he asked, twisting the cap off and tossing it into the plastic garbage pail.

Bobbi sat down on the living room chair closest to the tiny foyer and pulled off her shoes, wiggling her toes and making circles with her cramped feet.

"Don't they live in Fairfax? I mean, it would seem you would want to at least visit them when you're here."

"I usually do," he answered, folding his lengthy frame onto the couch. Taking a healthy swig of the beer, he leaned back and stretched one arm along the back of it. "They're not here right now, though. Left two weeks ago for a month in Europe."

Bobbi sighed and slumped wearily in her own chair. "That would be nice. Just to get away for a month...

no time clocks to punch...no car pools...no waking up at five thirty every morning.''

Her wistful expression did not escape Blain's attention. ''Don't you like your job?'' he asked, not as a challenge but in honest curiosity.

''Of course I do,'' Bobbi answered defiantly. ''I've worked very hard to get the position I'm in now.''

''And you're discovering it's not all it was cut out to be.''

Bobbi's eyes narrowed. ''You're putting words in my mouth.''

Blain cocked one eyebrow knowingly. ''But you don't deny it.''

Bobbi's frown eased and she chewed on her lower lip thoughtfully for a moment before answering. ''Well, in some respects I don't...I guess.'' The truth of the matter was, she'd never really taken the time to analyze her feelings concerning her job, she'd been so wrapped up in it. 'I don't really know why I said that.'' She spoke her thoughts aloud. ''I—I just—''

Blain set the beer bottle down on a wooden coaster. ''You're just suffering from classical burnout,'' he finished for her.

His omniscient tone rankled her, and Bobbi glared at him from beneath hooded eyes. ''And what would *you* know about *that*?''

Crossing the ankle of one leg across the knee of the other, Blain appeared to give the question some thought, then stated quietly, ''Oh...I'm not so unfamiliar with the syndrome myself.'' His gaze focused on her disbelieving one for a second, then shifted to study some undefined point beyond her shoulder.

His last statement held a note of sincerity Bobbi could not ignore. She studied him for a moment, curious at this seemingly different side of Blain Pearson, a side she simply could not, at that point, sympathize with in the least.

"I would have thought playing professional basketball and making all that money would satisfy your every need and desire. What more could you want?"

Blain merely blinked in response. Bobbi wasn't sure he'd even heard her. Was he thinking back on some other position he'd held before becoming a professional athlete? she speculated. Despite the urge to refrain from showing any undue interest, curiosity took hold. "So how long have you been playing pro basketball?"

Blain lifted his eyebrows and rubbed the bridge of his nose with his thumb and forefinger. "Ten years."

"That's a long time."

"Yeah. Sometimes it seems like ten days. Sometimes like a hundred years."

Bobbi frowned slightly as she asked, "Is that good or bad?"

Blain chuckled lightly. "I don't have any regrets, if that's what you mean. It's been a very big part of me. My whole life almost."

"So how did you get into it?"

Blain smiled at her obvious interest, so unlike her usual stance of complete unconcern and almost dislike for his profession. "When you grow up looking like a bean pole, it's rather predictable that someone will try to push you in that direction."

Bean pole was hardly Bobbi's choice of description

for the handsome athlete sitting across from her, but she kept the thought to herself. "Is that what your parents did; push you into it?"

Blain shook his head. "Oh, no. They emphasized scholastics before sports. Always. No, a particularly enthusiastic coach took me under his wing when I was barely into high school. And I turned out to be pretty good."

"And college?"

"On scholarship to Duke." Blain smiled and his eyes glimmered with nostalgia. "I loved it there. The best years of my life...as they say."

"What was your major?" Bobbi asked.

"Political Science."

"Hmmm. Very interesting."

"Actually, it was. Very much so."

Both were silent then, each lost in their own particular thoughts and reminiscences. Bobbi's head was filled with images of a younger Blain Pearson, famous campus jock— No, she didn't want to think of that. In fact, she was devoting far too much time thinking about the man, period.

Hooking the crook of her finger in the heel straps of her sandals, she stood, her movement catching his attention. "I think I'll take a nap before we leave for supper," she said.

Blain nodded. "Sure. I thought we'd leave around seven."

"That sounds fine," Bobbi agreed, then walked through the hallway to her bedroom, feeling an overwhelming need just then to get away from him for a couple of precious hours.

The early spring could get quite nippy in the evenings, and Bobbi kept that fact in mind as she studied the contents of her closet for the most suitable attire for that evening. Her pale green silk dress and matching jacket would do nicely, she decided.

Her nap had refreshed her considerably, but grips of hunger pains were becoming more and more frequent by the time she and Blain got into the car, Blain once again taking the wheel.

The conversation they shared on the rather lengthy ride was low-key, interspersed with periodic silences as the lush beauty of the surrounding countryside they were traveling through captured their attention. The two-lane highway skirted miles of rolling verdant hunt country, the fading dusk light tinging all with a soft violet hue. Horses dotted the sloping pastures, their heads bent, grazing on the rich grass in peaceful contentment.

Blain turned off the highway onto a gravel road that narrowed down to a one-car width as it led onto a wooden bridge spanning a sparsely filled creek. Bobbi wondered at the unfamiliar direction they were taking and gave voice to her curiosity.

"Don't worry," Blain reassured her, "this is the back way to the restaurant. I thought you might appreciate the scenery."

And indeed it was impossible not to do just that. The drive through the lush forest was truly worth every bump and lurch of the car. Evergreens lent a rich green backdrop to the young blooms of spruces and maples and oak trees. Bobbi relished the untouched loveliness of the place; she could well imagine being there in another day and time, taking the trip in a horse-drawn buggy.

As the road left the forest it became paved once more, and the car resumed a more comfortable motion. Bobbi's attention was glued to the surrounding countryside, and it occurred to her that she had become so ensconced in her tiny workaday world that she had completely forgotten the wondrous beauty that was so near her home. Did the same thing happen to most people? she wondered with a tinge of sadness at the thought.

Blain turned the car into the wide curving drive in front of the restaurant, a renovated eighteenth-century mansion, its red-brick front walls supported by enormous white columns. Roses competed with a variety of spring blossoms in a carefully tended garden that flanked the walkway leading up to the entrance; a virtual riot of color, the blossoms exuded a heady, exotic perfume into the night air. Inside, care had been taken to preserve the original Early American decor, the actual dining rooms integrated so well with each room of the rambling house that there was absolutely no mistaking the original function of each.

Blain exchanged a few words with the manager of the restaurant, the old friend he'd spoken of earlier, and immediately he and Bobbi were led to the back part of the mansion's lower floor. They were seated near a glass wall that separated the enclosed veranda from the sweeping lawn beyond.

"This is absolutely gorgeous," Bobbi whispered in awe as she gazed out upon the skillfully landscaped vista, her eyes scanning the rapidly darkening silhouette of the distant mountains, the oblong shape of a golden-crested hill in full splendid view.

"That's Sugarloaf," Blain said, his gaze following hers.

"Fantastic," Bobbi murmured. "I've seen it from a distance often enough, but seeing it this close up is marvelous."

"I thought you'd agree. The backyard-like view is one of the major reasons for the original location of this place...and for its success now."

Bobbi's expression bespoke an almost childlike innocence, a refreshingly delightful reaction that bordered on fascination. The softly lit room cast a golden glow across her delicate features; the pale green silk of her dress lent an emerald depth to her eyes. She was wearing her hair in a different fashion that night; brushed back away from her forehead, it cascaded down about her neck and the tops of her shoulders in free-flowing cinnamon-brown curls. Blain's hands clutched in agitation, suppressing the urge to reach out and caress the ample locks, to feel the texture of her face and throat, so like, he was sure, the silken material of her dress.

She spoke just then, a shade of embarrassment reflected in her tone. "You didn't have to go to this much trouble just to take me out to dinner."

Blain shrugged his wide shoulders and grinned. "Why not? I wanted to do it." He paused. "I'm sure you've been treated in similar fashion before. By former lovers perhaps?"

Bobbi cast him an arch look. "And what makes you assume I've had former lovers?"

Again Blain shrugged. "It just seems rather unlikely that you haven't," he stated simply.

Bobbi would have retorted immediately, but on second thought decided that silence would be a better response. What harm would it do if he chose to think of her as more worldy and sophisticated than she could claim to be?

Instead she cocked one eyebrow and asked, "And what about you? How many past—or present—lovers do you claim?"

Blain chuckled lightly and nodded to the waiter who had just handed them menus and the wine list. Indicating that they would prefer a few moments to study both, Blain answered, "Too many to remember."

Bobbi smiled, then studied his face for a moment, wondering how much truth there was to that offhand statement. Plenty, most likely.

But then, the consideration was merely an academic one; what possible difference could Blain Pearson's past *or* present romantic life mean to her anyway?

The cuisine lived up to its reputation, Bobbi discovered. Her appetite found exquisite appeasement in the succulent roast duck, wild rice, and a selection of delicately seasoned sauces. The wine, a hearty, yet mellow Burgundy, provided the perfect complement to the meal. As the evening progressed Bobbi's mood lightened considerably. Little by little she found herself letting down her guard against her weekend intruder. Once, when he unexpectedly reached out and took her hand in his, it seemed a quite natural gesture, and she made no objection whatsoever. She stared down at her small slender hand captured within his large hair-roughened one and found it somehow impossible to even attempt escape. In truth, she would not have been displeased to have it stay there for the remainder of the evening. But then an uncontrollable shiver coursed the length of her arm as Blain's thumb began tracing a slow circular pattern along the tender, sensitive flesh of her inner wrist. Her heart responded to this expert maneuver as well, she discovered shortly, thumping its erratic beat against her chest wall, her pulse racing along to keep pace. Quickly she withdrew her hand, and when Blain eyed her curiously for a moment, she hid her loss of composure by reaching down at her side for her clutch bag, then politely excusing herself for a moment to visit the ladies' room.

Once there, Bobbi could only hope that the flushed, disquieted visage staring back at her had not been visible in the muted lighting of the restaurant. She'd simply drunk too much wine, she chastised herself. Certainly it hadn't been Blain who had produced those intoxicating currents of sensual sensations stirring in her blood. Of all the men in the world to whom she would have thought herself to be attracted, Blain Pearson was most definitely the least practical. The two of them shared nothing in common. She possessed absolutely no interest whatsoever in sports, even as a spectator, and most especially the sport of professional basketball. Her college years had not left her with a favorable impression of athletic sorts either; shunted through the process of higher education on scholarships, most of the jocks she'd known, including the very few whom she'd had the unfortunate experience of dating, had simply been passed through their courses. Definitely not her type. How many times had she reminded herself of that in the past forty-eight hours? she wondered with more than a touch of chagrin.

No, Bobbi shook her head determinedly, her reaction that evening was attributable to the wine alone. She wasn't foolish enough to deny the physical attraction she felt for Blain; she had recognized and admitted that fact from the beginning. But her reliable common sense and pragmatic approach to most things, including her romantic life, had prevailed this far...as it would, of course, in the future. Besides, any further weakening on her part posed no real problem anyway; by Monday the problem with Blain's car would be taken care of, and he would be gone from her life.

Somehow that thought was not quite as comforting as she would have expected it to be. Frowning slightly, Bobbi fussed with her hair for a few lingering moments, rationalizing the confusing feeling, then returned to the dining room.

The ride home seemed much shorter than the trip there—but then, that was always the case when going somewhere for the first time, Bobbi reflected. The combination of rich food and wine, plus the lulling motion of the car, caused Bobbi's eyes to droop wearily, and gradually she gave in to the drowsiness, her body slumping toward the console.

Blain looked down at the dozing woman beside him and experienced a distinct tug at his heart. She was so tiny, so fragile...so vulnerable. Yet he knew only too

well the fireball personality temporarily hidden behind the innocent visage. Oddly it seemed to be that
combination, the crazy mixture of sugar and pepper,
that attracted him to her so.

Keeping his left hand on the steering wheel, his
right gently touched her outside shoulder, his fingers
stroking in soft, quiet circles the silk material of her
dress. The faintly vanilla fragrance she wore stirred
him more than he could ever recall, and with utmost
concentration he kept his attention on the darkened
stretch of freeway along which they were traveling.

Bobbi awoke suddenly as the car jolted mildly as it
rolled across a speed bump in the apartment parking
lot. Involuntarily she sucked in her breath as her eyes
blinked open, more surprised at the position she
found herself in than the fact that she really had slept
most of the way home. The left side of her face was
tingling numbly from its position against Blain's arm,
and her right shoulder responded to the pressure of
his hand. How in the world?... She had either slid
over his way—across the console, at that!—or he had
positioned her so. Nevertheless the position was disturbingly comfortable. Groggily she sat up straighter,
and Blain removed his arm, using both hands now to
maneuver the car into her parking space.

As she waited for Blain to come around to her side
of the car, Bobbi's conscience waged a debate over
what had just occurred. She had absolutely no intention whatsoever of allowing a physical relationship to
develop between the two of them, and she certainly
hoped he had not gotten that impression. But then,
she really had no idea whether or not she was to

blame for the position she'd found herself in. She'd simply been guilty of falling asleep in the car; how she came to rest so near Blain was a matter only he knew of, and she was not about to ask him about it.

As she stepped out of the car Blain's hand slipped firmly beneath her upper arm as he locked, then shut, the door. In spite of her better judgment she made no protest as he pulled her closer to his side, leading her across the parking lot toward the apartment complex. They walked in silence, and after Blain unlocked the door to her apartment, Bobbi entered ahead of him, switching on the foyer light and opening the small entry closet.

She hung up her jacket and turned to ask Blain if she might do the same with his jacket. He was mere inches from her, she discovered quickly, and a slight gasp escaped her parted lips as suddenly she found herself within the circle of his arms. He smiled languidly down at her, and a searing sensation darted through her abdomen like a high-voltage current. Automatically her body stiffened, overwhelmed by the confusing emotions wreaking havoc on her better judgment. She wanted to pull away, to run from him, but simultaneously she felt every nerve fiber, every muscle tendon, straining to feel more distinctly the length of the hard, potent form claiming her so.

Her lips parted even more, summoning words that stubbornly refused to be spoken. Blain, however, relieved her of the necessity as he half spoke, half whispered, his sensuous tone fanning the sparks of desire within her to a leaping flame.

"I want to thank you," he said in a low, even tone.

"F-for . . . what?" she murmured breathlessly.

"For such a wonderful evening. It was quite a change for me. One I've needed for a long, long time." His arms slid up the slender length of her back then, one hand continuing upward to her nape, gently pushing aside the curtain of cinnamon-colored hair. Druggingly his palm and thumb massaged the sensitive cord of her upper spine.

The movement had a two-fold effect on Bobbi; its methodic motion instantly brought her resistance to a melting point, at the same time pushing her off-balance, making it necessary for her to take a step forward, their bodies pressing firmly together then.

For an instant Bobbi felt some inner self standing aside, watching as her sensible defenses rapidly faded beneath the powerful allure of this physical contact. Desperately she searched for some meaningful reply to his words, some strength to pull her back into the realm of reality and control over the situation.

"I find that rather hard to believe," she said finally, practically gulping. Her eyes found it easier to rest on his evening-shadowed chin instead of the all-too-penetrating blue eyes studying her face, her lips, in such intimate measure. "I would have thought this would be rather a routine event for you."

"And why would you think that?" His hand traveled along the side of her neck, his thumb tracing slow, nerve-tingling circles just below her ear.

Bobbi drew in a calming breath, but it was ragged and pitifully ineffective. "Surely you don't expect me to think you lead a celibate life, Mr. Pearson," she managed to counter with a touch of sarcasm.

"And you?" Blain whispered softly, his head lowering terribly close to her own now. "Am I to believe you're the innocent virgin awaiting her knight on a white steed?"

Under any other circumstances, she would have considered the cliché ridiculously, laughably trite, but her reaction then was intensely felt as Bobbi found herself blushing furiously. However, any verbal response she would have summoned up was quickly squelched as he took total advantage of her momentary speechlessness.

Her full, slightly trembling lips were just as he'd imagined they'd be, tautly resisting at first, then warming gradually to a soft pliancy under the patient nibbling of his own, eventually parting to reveal the sweet depths within. Encircled in his arms, her supple body was fragile, yet firm, and he longed to lift her, to gather her up to a more convenient level. Slowly, carefully, his arms slid down around her back, the sensuous massage that had begun on her neck continuing in more exploring patterns along the column of her spine. With an uncontrollable groan, he pressed her closer to him, the passion kindling within his chest exploding to a blazing inferno as Bobbi responded, the flat of her palms pressing against his back as she hungered too for the feel of him, a muffled gasp of urgency escaping her throat as her own physical excitement became apparent. What followed was the most natural thing in the world to Bobbi's enflamed senses. Their mouths still clinging, Blain lifted her like a baby, her weight a totally negligible matter, and carried her to the couch. The room was dark, the only illumination that of the light still on in the foyer.

Bobbi lay on his lap, the back of her head in the crook of his arm, her body half turned toward his. The kiss was never-ending, and as Blain's hand began to glide across her back and down her spine in smooth, nerve-tingling strokes, Bobbi writhed even closer to him.

She was drowning within his arms, the hand caressing her eliciting an unbelievable depth of sensation throughout her entire body. The smell of him taunted her, and she reached out to touch, then squeeze, the rippling stone-hard muscles of his arm. Blain's free hand had a mind of its own; covering one breast with its palm, he began a sensuous, drugging massage like none other Bobbi had ever experienced. Her back arched toward him, inviting him further, challenging the tiny warning voice within her. But she didn't care what it was saying... didn't want to hear it. Until she felt that same hand moving slowly across her stomach. and leg, sliding beneath the silken dress, fingers pressing firmly upward along her inner thigh.

Something inside Bobbi's head reacted instantly; the warning voice had won. Her eyes, which had remained closed, blinked rapidly in dawning awareness of her loss of control. Bringing her hands up between their bodies, she pushed against Blain's chest. Suddenly panicky, she twisted, then pulled, her mouth back from the burning possession of his, finally breaking free just enough to gasp, "Please, Blain...no."

"No what?" he rasped, his lips finding solace, for the moment, along her smooth brow.

"Don't...it's not right," Bobbi protested feebly, swallowing spasmodically.

"What's not right?" His voice was heavy, laden with passionate tension.

"Do you have to answer every question with another?" she said exasperatedly. Jerkily she reached down and pulled his hand away, smoothing the dress back over her legs. Reluctantly he released her, and with an embarrassingly awkward movement, she clambered off the couch, standing well away from him in the darkened room. Her voice was difficult to summon and she spoke in a raspy tone. "Have you forgotten your promise when I agreed to let you stay here for the weekend? You assured me you had no ulterior motives."

Blain sighed lengthily as he spread his arms along the back of the couch. "Is that what you call what just happened? *My* ulterior motives? What about your own?"

Bobbi frowned. "What kind of remark is that?"

"An honest one. I got the impression you were rather enjoying yourself."

Bobbi's lips compressed into a grimace and she replied hotly, "This was all *your* idea, dammit. I'm not a robot. I never claimed to be. *But,* Mr. Pearson, let me make this perfectly clear: I had no intention whatsoever of allowing anything physical to happen between us. And," she added firmly, "believe me, it won't happen again. I'm not in the habit of doling out sexual favors like—like the sort of woman I'm sure you're used to. If that's all you need, then"—she took a step forward and switched on a lamp, then flung an arm out dramatically—"you're welcome to use my telephone. I'm sure your floozy blond 'tenant' would be more than happy to respond to your beck and call."

She sounded like some enraged vixen, but inexplicably the mere thought of his doing what she had just suggested fired her anger even more. And all too aware of the dangerous flare of temper threatening to spew forth, she hurriedly snatched up her purse from the foyer and moved toward the hallway.

"And, oh... thanks for the dinner," she said tightly, unable to control the waver in her tone. "I'm going to bed now."

Blain's expression was carefully blank as he simply stared at her.

Turning on her heels, Bobbi began to stalk off toward her bedroom.

"Bobbi?"

She stopped, not bothering to turn back around. "Yes?"

"Good night...sleep tight."

Bobbi bit her inside lower lip almost painfully but made no response as she walked into her bedroom, shutting the door firmly behind her and turning the lock.

Chapter Seven

Three staccato raps on the door awakened Bobbi from her restless state of early morning sleep. Her eyes opened halfway and she threw one arm across her forehead as she called out hoarsely, "Yes?"

"I just wanted to let you know, I'm taking your keys to the car. I'll be back in a few minutes." He certainly sounds wide-awake, Bobbi thought resentfully. Good Lord, was he like that every morning?

"Where are you going?" she asked, raising up on her elbows and yawning widely.

"In case you've forgotten, you have nothing left in the refrigerator ... or in the pantry. I thought I'd make a quick run down to McDonald's and pick up some breakfast."

In spite of herself Bobbi rolled her eyes heavenward.

Christ, he was something else! Rip-roaring and ready to eat at that hour of the morning.

"All right," she answered, flipping onto her side, her eyelids closing wearily as she listened to him leaving the apartment. In less than twenty-four hours, she

reminded herself, she would have her apartment—
and her life—to herself.

Bobbi swallowed deeply. Her eyelids snapped open
suddenly and she found herself staring blankly at the
wall opposite the bed. Strange... there was no reason
for the unexpected tenseness that seized her then.
Surely she could make it through the rest of the weekend. Yes, of course she could.

But that wasn't really the issue, was it? No, Bobbi
admitted ruefully, the fact of the matter was that
Blain's leaving was affecting her in an altogether
unexpected way. Incredibly his presence there had
started to grow on her in a surprising, yet rather comfortable manner. A barrage of hunger pains assaulted
her just then, as if on cue.... He had even effected a
major change in her appetite!

The memory of the previous night's encounter entered her thoughts just then, a pointed reminder that
something far deeper had developed in regard to her
feelings for Blain. She'd managed to soothe the troubled realization of the night before with assurances
that her reaction was due mainly to the effects of the
rich food and the heady wine. And, of course, she had
feelings like everyone else... physical feelings, which,
by choice, had perhaps been left unattended far too
long. It was only natural that she should respond to
his kiss the way she had. She winced, remembering
how obvious she must have appeared responding so
readily, almost eagerly.

But of course she realized that what Blain Pearson
thought of her responsiveness was inconsequential
really. Undoubtedly what had happened last night was

only mildly entertaining compared to his routine conquests. Oh, he'd perhaps been somewhat irritated that he'd gotten no further than he had, but he'd obviously forgotten about it, from the sound of his voice this morning.

Agitatedly Bobbi sat up, pushed the covers down to the lower end of the bed, and brought her legs up, wrapping her arms about them and resting her chin atop her knees. What was *really* the issue was her silly reaction to the entire situation. What she had thought would be a weekend that, for wiser purposes, she would simply have to endure was rapidly turning into an emotional fiasco. She felt almost...*afraid* somehow. But afraid of what? Afraid of being alone again after he left? That was ridiculous. She'd been managing by herself quite well up to that point. It seemed ludicrous that she should have lost the ability to cope in one short weekend spent with a man she hardly even knew. Oddly enough she couldn't help admitting that she really didn't feel that way about him. On the contrary, it seemed as if she'd known him for a very long while. In spite of everything—the real reason for his even being there, the fact that she was no more than another potential conquest for him—Bobbi had to admit that for some reason his presence in her life seemed almost natural. No man she had ever known had even come close to having such an effect on Bobbi Morrow.

What was it she had promised herself a long time ago? she asked herself. That she wouldn't make the same mistakes her friends, scores of them, had made by marrying the first person they thought themselves to be in love with, then succumbing to the high divorce rate that afflicted such young marriages. Bobbi too had fallen in love during her college years, but she had survived the temptation to follow like another of the meek flock, delivering herself upon the sacrificial altar of marriage.

It wasn't that she didn't believe in marriage either. She did, very much so; but a different type of marriage, one not simply for show but for real, for a lifetime. She was all too aware how corny the ideal would sound to others, therefore she had simply adopted a professed disinterest in the subject, unwilling to expose her sensitive feelings.

So what did her lofty, boring ideals have to do with Blain Pearson? Everything and nothing, she answered truthfully. She was painfully aware that she was physically attracted to him, and given a lesser willpower than she possessed, last night could have easily led to far greater acquiescence on her part. Yet try as she might to live with the times, to accept the fulfillment of her needs and wants on a more casual, convenient basis, she just couldn't.

She stared blankly at the foot of the bed, her mind void for a few precious moments of any further thoughts on the subject. Then, with an audible sigh, she shoved herself off the bed and slid her feet into her slippers. She may as well avail herself of Blain's absence by taking her turn in the bathroom.

Standing before the mirror, she studied her vision as she brushed her teeth. The unmade-up eyes staring back at her held a shadow of cynicism as the subject of her feelings toward Blain Pearson sprang back into full consideration. Was all this conjecture, in fact, simply a waste of time and speculation? Wasn't she making a mountain out of a molehill by even giving the situation that much thought? After all, she reminded herself, he'd be leaving the following morning, and none of it would make one iota of difference after that.

The testing of Bobbi's true feelings concerning Blain's departure arrived, it seemed, with undue haste. She awakened Monday morning, at her usual ungodly before-dawn hour, with a nagging headache, memories of the weekend still painfully fresh.

After Blain's return yesterday morning, the remainder of the day had seemed to fly by. He'd made no mention of their Saturday night passion, and Bobbi was both relieved and somewhat perturbed that he'd apparently forgotten it so easily. That fact only confirmed her earlier suspicion that it had been of far less significance to him than to her.

However, Blain had been in an amusing, lighthearted mood, and Bobbi's conflicting emotions were soon pushed to the back of her conscious state of mind.

They had left for the Capital Centre before noon, and once there, Blain had taken pains to see that Bobbi had a choice seat for the game. Once again her reaction had been surprisingly uncharacteristic. She'd found herself becoming completely involved, her initial feeling of isolation rapidly overshadowed by the growing excitement of the home crowd surrounding her. Once an uninvolved outsider, she quickly became swept up in the noise and cheer, contributing a healthy amount of yelling and shouting herself, understanding a good deal more of the game than she would have given herself credit for.

The game itself, however, was not the entire reason for Bobbi's sudden enthusiasm for the sport. Try as she might to avoid it, her gaze constantly found itself drawn to one particular figure down on the court: Blain Pearson. She watched in fascination as his long, lean body continually wheeled and spun and raced along the court, his bronze muscular body a virtual machine of skill and concentration. It seemed hard to believe that the man she was watching then was the same easygoing, almost domesticated male she had shared the weekend with. Blain Pearson obviously possessed many more facets to his enigmatic personality than she had yet been witness to.

Bobbi and Blain had gone out to dinner after the game to a restaurant in the near vicinity. The restaurant lacked the rustic, historical charm of the one they'd dined at the night before, but it possessed a definite ambiance of its own. The conversation had revolved around basketball; the Bullets had won, though in the first three quarters they'd trailed by an almost constant five to fifteen points. By the fourth quarter they had gotten their act together and they'd finally penetrated the Lakers' defense to pull out ahead with a burst of scoring that had the home crowd screaming ecstatically. Blain was high on the victory...nothing could keep them down that year, he claimed.

"Do you think the Bullets have a chance at the championship?" Bobbi asked. They'd both finished a

satisfying meal and were lingering over the remainder
of a bottle of wine.

"Without a doubt," Blain answered readily. "This
should be the year, if we can keep it together the way
we have been."

Bobbi sipped delicately at her wine, then looked at
Blain over the rim of the glass. As she placed it back
down she asked, "Is it very important to you; winning
the championship?"

Blain looked at her with an expression of incredulity. "Of course it's important. It always is."

A certain intensity glazed over his deep blue eyes
for a second, and Bobbi wondered if perhaps there
was more to the pat answer. She seemed to have lost
him for a moment, and it was confusing...a piece of
the puzzle of Blain Pearson she hadn't known was
missing. She started to say something more when
Blain's gaze shifted to the restaurant entrance. Bobbi
turned at the sound of a crowd of voices and then
recognized several of his teammates with their wives
and their dates. Within seconds, it seemed, the quiet
intimacy she and Blain had shared was shattered as
Blain extended an invitation for everyone to join
them at a larger table that was found for all of them.

The next couple of hours were, for Bobbi, an absolute trial of patience and inordinate restraint. She
didn't know these people...hadn't asked to know
them, and resentment mounted toward Blain for having thrown her into the situation without even con-
sulting her.

But the experience was enlightening in one respect:
it was an excellent opportunity to observe Blain in the

element in which he was most at home and most often involved; an element she had absolutely nothing in common with, nor had any desire for—All of which only served to confirm her inner conviction that she and Blain were at opposite ends of the spectrum as far as life-styles went. He seemed to thrive on the companionship of his teammates; after all, he spent ninety percent of his life around them. With a growing feeling of discomfort and a definite desire to get away from them all, Bobbi survived the evening, supremely relieved when Blain finally suggested it was time they call it a night.

They both were more than a little weary by the time they reached the apartment, and when Blain switched on the television, they settled down on opposite ends of the couch to watch a thirties Lombard and Mac-Murray film.

Bobbi was grateful for the distance he respected for the length of the movie, but for some ridiculous reason she found Blain's acceptance of the situation strangely irritating. Apparently the raucous evening with his friends had completely erased the ardor he'd exhibited the previous night. But that was just as well . . . she had no room for it herself anyway.

As she struggled to arise Monday morning Bobbi sighed wearily, shoved her fingers through her hair, and rubbed her aching temples in slow circular motions, thinking of her previous assessment of yesterday. The good time they'd shared—before the tiresome affair with his friends—was probably just that to Blain; a good time. She had no doubt he enjoyed being with her more than he'd counted on when dreaming up his little revenge plot, but it was fairly obvious that what minor physical enjoyment he had sampled he could just as easily do without. Surely there were others to take care of his every need in that department.

Well, fine! Bobbi growled inwardly, jerking the bedroom door open and walking through the hallway to the bathroom, not taking any great pains to subdue the noise she made in the effort. She opened and shut drawers with careless abandon, and the water pipes whined and sang out loudly as she started the shower.

Emerging from the bathroom several minutes later, she discovered that her noisiness hadn't disturbed Blain Pearson in the least. He still slept soundly on her couch, looking like an overgrown little boy with the covers gathered up around his chin, his bare feet protruding over the opposite end of the couch. Bobbi stood for a moment in the doorway, crossing her arms over her chest and shaking her head in rueful amazement. *Nothing* bothers the man! she thought enviously, resenting his laid-back attitude, which seemed to color every aspect of his life.

"Time to get up," she called out loudly, walking briskly toward the kitchen to prepare a pot of coffee. Her traitorous stomach growled in expectation of a meal, but she was all too aware that it would receive no appeasement that morning, since she still hadn't been able to restock her pantry or her refrigerator. Thanks to *him* she would have to deal with hunger pains in the morning, something she'd never experienced before in her life!

Blain groaned and turned onto his side, his eyes remaining closed as Bobbi stirred about in the kitchen. "Aha!" Bobbi commented, filling up the glass coffeepot with water and measuring out the appropriate amount of grounds into the automatic coffee brewer. "So you're not as alert in the mornings as you've pretended to be."

"Wha—" came the muffled reply from the couch.

"I *said*," Bobbi drawled out slowly, "it seems you're not as wide-awake and rarin' to go as you've pretended to be in the morning. But then"—she let the cabinet door slam as she extracted cream and sugar—"that was probably because you were able to get up so late. But us working class folk aren't so fortunate, you see. We have to get up with the roosters, if you'll pardon the expression."

Blain remained sprawled out on the couch, his mouth contorted lopsidedly as it lay flush across his arm. Bobbi walked back into the living room, determined that he get up. There wasn't that much time before they had to leave, and she assumed he'd want to shower first. For a moment she stood next to him, her hands on her hips and her arms akimbo, as she considered just how in the world she was going to get such a hulk of a man up. He obviously was either ignoring her or had fallen back asleep. Her gaze focused for a second on one size fourteen foot peeping out the end of the blanket, and her eyes narrowed devilishly. Then, without further hesitation, she reached out and grabbed the little toe, yanking it hard as she reminded him sharply, "Time to get up, sleepyhead!"

The ruse worked perfectly, though somewhat alarm-

ingly, Bobbi discovered, as she jumped back the instant
Blain jolted upright, propping himself up on bent elbows.

"Ouch!" he exclaimed, jerking his long leg back
immediately. Bobbi felt a gurgle of laughter rise up as
she took in the sight of him, his hair askance and
falling haphazardly around his face, his expression so
reminiscent of a little boy's, churlish and unhappy at
the rude awakening.

"What are you trying to do?" he barked at her, and
Bobbi was almost glad to see him angered; for once he
wasn't the perfect, even-tempered character he'd
shown himself to be.

"I'm trying," Bobbi said exasperatedly as she
moved toward the hallway well out of his range, "to
get you up! We have to leave soon."

"What for?" Blain rubbed his eyes and slid his
hand down to rub against his itchy growth of beard.
"What time is it?"

"It's almost seven o'clock, and since I'm sure you
don't want to get caught in the morning traffic, which
I assure you has already begun, then you'll have to get
up so we can get going."

"Where are we going?"

Bobbi half closed her bedroom door as she slipped
into a blouse and a skirt, raising her voice somewhat
for it to carry into the living room.

"I'm going to work, dummy," she answered. "And
you only have a few hours before your flight, in case
you forgot. But first we have to stop by the holding lot
and get your car."

Mention of his Corvette apparently did the trick.

Bobbi could hear Blain trekking into the kitchen, fumbling around in her cabinet for a mug into which to pour himself some coffee.

"You'll have to skip breakfast this morning," Bobbi called out. "I don't have anything to fix, and we don't have time anyway."

He made no reply, but she was fairly certain she heard some sort of sour grunt as he opened and shut the refrigerator, then the pantry, as if to assure himself of the fact.

As Bobbi set about making her bed and gathering her things together, she was gratified to hear that Blain had at least made his way into the bathroom and was in the process of showering. Minutes later the steady hum of her electric razor could be heard as he shaved. *That* was one thing she would welcome back as soon as he left. Since, as he'd reminded her frequently, his own toiletry items were locked away in the trunk of his car, which she'd impounded, he was without a razor of his own. Bobbi had begrudgingly added that to the list of the many things she had shared with him that weekend.

When he emerged from the bathroom, Bobbi was dismayed to see that he had only his socks and slacks on and was in the process of towel-drying his hair.

"*What* are you doing?" she asked, more than a touch of annoyance in her tone.

Blain's hand, which moved the towel in smooth forward and backward drying strokes, stopped as he answered, "Drying my hair."

"But why did you have to wash it?" Bobbi almost wailed. "We have to get going soon. I *don't* want to be late for work and I'm going to be if you don't hurry up and get dressed."

"All right, all right. Where's your dryer?" Blain tossed the towel back into the bathroom and took his shirt off its hanger, putting it on as he slipped his feet into his shoes. Bobbi, growing more agitated by the second, sighed disgustedly and stalked into the bathroom, opened the linen closet door, and reached for the blow-dryer she kept there.

Blain was still buttoning his shirt as she marched past him to the dining room table. "Come over here," she stated, bending over to plug the cord of the dryer into the dining room wall outlet.

"What for?" Blain asked, sauntering over and frowning at her curious action.

Bobbi glanced pointedly at her watch and repeated, "Just come over here, dammit!"

Blain's lips curved upward in a surprised grin. "Okay, okay." He complied, moving toward her.

"Now sit down."

Blain raised his shoulders in mock surrender and he sat down as she indicated.

"We'll never get going on time if you just take forever like this." With a flip of the switch, the blow-dryer began blasting warm, then hot, air over Blain's wet locks, Bobbi helping the process along by running her fingers through the thick mass of auburn hair, simultaneously shaping and hastening the drying process.

Blain couldn't have been more pleased with her insistence on drying his hair. He was none too good at it himself and more often than not ended up by simply leaving his hair half wet. The fact that he wouldn't be exposing his damp head to the fresh, cool morning air was secondary, though, to the pleasure he was experiencing from Bobbi's delicate fingers stroking his sensitive scalp. The effect was almost hypnotizing, and he slid down in the chair a bit to better accommodate his height to the level of her arms, closing his eyes until she was finished.

Bobbi, on the other hand, was none too pleased with herself for making the offer. Had she known she would respond this way, she would have simply let him perform the chore himself, regardless of being late. It was something she could have done without, that was certain! As she held the dryer with her right hand her left fluffed and sculpted, her fingers lifting and pulling the thick burnished locks over his ears and down his nape. Her fingers reacted to the nearness of him with a mind of their own; the impulse to let them roam along the base of his neck, down the taut cord of his spine, around the strong, smoothly muscled throat was almost overwhelming. . . .

Then suddenly the steady drone of the instrument ceased as Blain reached up and switched it off. Bobbi was startled by the move, yet before she could object Blain turned fully around in the chair and in a swift, economical movement reached out and pulled her onto his lap, smothering her cry of protest by placing his firm, insistent lips upon her own. Unable to move, let alone escape the arms that pinioned her against him, Bobbi could only acquiesce to the demands of his willful kiss. Given the distracted state she was already in, it would have been difficult indeed to do otherwise.

Unconsciously she arched toward him, her breasts pressed flat against his chest. His tongue traveled tauntingly along the inner recesses of her mouth, darting challengingly against her own. With one hand he held the back of her neck, twisting her hair within large, strong fingers. His other hand moved slowly down one shoulder, massaging it in a drugging rhythm, the corner of his wrist resting against the side of her breast in burning familiarity.

Bobbi felt her heartbeat quicken, and her breath became ragged and broken. The physical reality of the situation suddenly jolted her mentally. What in God's name was she doing? With a tremendous burst of strength she jerked her head to the side, pushing her hands against him to free herself completely. She stumbled as she got to her feet and, embarrassed, turned and snatched up the blow-dryer and began wrapping the cord around the handle.

"You're not finished, are you?"

She could hear the amusement in Blain's tone and bristled inwardly as she answered curtly, "Yep."

"But my hair's still damp."

"It'll just have to air dry. We have to go now. As it is, I'll barely get to work on time." Her refusal to acknowledge what had just happened was painfully obvious and, angrily, she stalked off toward the bathroom, not daring to turn around and face the smugness she was certain was plastered all over his face.

By the time Bobbi returned to the living room Blain was slipping into his sport jacket.

"Are you ready?" she asked briskly, checking to making sure the kitchen and dining room lights were out.

"Ready as ever," Blain answered lightly.

"Good," Bobbi replied, avoiding the ocean-blue gaze studying her with obvious bemusement as she walked toward the front door and opened it. "Then, let's go."

"Belinda, are you sure?" Bobbi's half whisper bordered on a strangled cry of disbelief. She was standing inside Belinda Logan's office at AMAC's subsidiary leasing company in Arlington. They'd arrived a few minutes earlier after having been informed that Blain's Corvette had been shipped over from the holding lot to the leasing company as soon as it had arrived.

Belinda shrugged and raised her eyebrows. "I'm very sure," she said, bemused by Bobbi's distressed expression. "As I said, we had a call for a sports model. The Corvette was available, so we had it sent over immediately."

Bobbi wiped her hand across her mouth in agitation. Slowly she sat down on the edge of the chair across from Belinda's desk and closed her eyes. It was unreal! Blain would never believe her. He'd kill her! Not only had his car been mistakenly confiscated, it was probably halfway across the state of Virginia, leased for an indefinite period by a traveling computer salesman.

"There's no chance he'll bring it back in today? In the next day or two?"

Belinda sighed. "Well, he specified unlimited mileage, so I seriously doubt it." She hesitated and scratched the side of her neck. "Look, we can get to work on it right away and try to track him down. As soon as we get a hold of him we'll have him bring the car back in. That's all I can tell you for the moment."

Bobbi slumped and said nothing, her frustration evident on her grim features. Finally she said, "Okay, I guess you're right." She began walking toward the door but hesitated as she placed her hand on the knob. "Uh, Belinda, I—well, I'd appreciate it if you'd keep this one hushed up. In fact, I'd appreciate it more than you'll ever know."

Belinda smiled and nodded at the young woman. "I understand. Don't give it another thought."

"Thanks," Bobbi said, opening the door and stepping outside into the front lobby. She was certain, in that particularly agonizing moment, that she knew exactly how the Christians must have felt just before stepping into the arena with a single ferocious hungry lion.

Blain looked up from his perusal of a brochure as Bobbi walked toward him. He frowned, taken aback by the ashen appearance of her normally feisty visage. Immediately he knew something was wrong.

"What is it?" he asked, setting the brochure down on a nearby table and standing up.

Bobbi wished he hadn't done that; she felt infinitely more at ease talking to him while he was on her own eye level. Nervously her gaze shifted around the room, then back to him.

"Do you mind if we go outside to my car?" she asked politely. If there was going to be a scene, she'd rather have it in private. On the other hand, considering the probable enormity of Blain's reaction, her health would no doubt be in far less danger if she stayed there.

Blain frowned slightly in confusion but he agreed, and together they walked outside to Bobbi's car. Inside, she nervously rummaged through her purse, a desperate, though useless, attempt to delay what had to be said.

"All right, what's up?" Blain asked. He had turned in the passenger seat to face her and his arms looked absolutely powerful crossed against his formidable chest.

Bobbi's eyes flitted about for a moment, then she drew in a deep breath and let it out with a rush of words, explaining why Blain's car was not there and what had happened.

Blain's reaction astonished her, and she regarded him warily, as if at any moment he might explode. Instead he continued to grin lopsidedly, his eyes narrowed in an expression of what could almost be termed amusement.

"You're something else," he said, shaking his head from side to side slowly. "This is just the sort of thing I expected might happen. I mean, what else could, right?"

"I—" Bobbi gulped. "I'm really sorry," she said, wincing painfully. "God, if I'd had any idea—"

"I know, I know," Blain interrupted. He gave a short sigh. "So how long do you think it'll be before the guy turns up?"

Encouraged by his truly calm reaction, Bobbi said in

a lighter tone, "Oh, I'm sure within the week. I'll do everything to see that this is put on top priority."

Blain scratched his forehead. "Well . . . I guess you'll have to give me a lift to the airport."

Bobbi clucked her tongue exasperatedly. "Yeah, I guess so. First, though, I'll have to run back inside and phone my office."

As she reached for the handle of the door Blain placed a restraining hand on her forearm. "Just a second," he said, smiling slyly. Quickly he snatched the keys from her, and Bobbi watched in dismay as he flipped through them until locating a silver one, identical to a gold one, the key to her apartment. Bobbi almost spluttered as he began sliding it off the circular holder.

"Blain . . . what are you doing?"

The key made a snapping noise as it came off, and Blain grinned and opened his eyes innocently as he closed his hand over it.

"The least I deserve, don't you think?"

Bobbi stared disbelievingly at him. "Surely you're kidding."

"Not in the least," Blain asserted gaily.

Suddenly believing him, Bobbi's hand shot out in an attempt to snatch the key from him, but Blain's reflexes were adept as usual and he swiftly pocketed the key.

"Give it back, dammit!" Bobbi's tone was seething.

"Oh, I don't think that's such a great idea. For you, that is."

Bobbi's eyes narrowed and she shot back between clenched teeth, "What does that mean?"

Blain had positioned an arm on the opened window ledge and began tapping his fingers on the rooftop. The sound only further irritated Bobbi, and it was all she could do to keep from lunging at him.

"I'm sure you'd rather we keep this little 'mistake' under our hats, too, wouldn't you?"

Bobbi's tone lowered as she responded, "Is that supposed to be a threat?"

Blain merely raised his eyebrows and shrugged.

Realizing the absolute futility of any further objections, Bobbi cast him one final glare before jerking open the car door. "You're a real jerk, Pearson," she hurled at him, only to hear his amused chuckle.

I should have known, she thought furiously, practically stomping back into the leasing office to make the necessary phone call. Leave it to Blain Pearson to pull something like that. God, why did she have to go and screw up with someone like him? She'd probably end up paying for that one mistake for the rest of her life.

Chapter Eight

Bobbi stared unseeingly at the contents of the open folder lying in front of her. With a silent groan she propped both elbows on her desk and rubbed her throbbing temples. The headache she'd started out with that morning had grown to a full-scale migraine. She glanced at her watch. Maybe lunch would help. Grudgingly she admitted that Blain may have been right. Perhaps she should have eaten breakfast that morning as she had with him during the weekend, but then, she'd never had a problem before....

"Oh, what's the use?" she muttered to herself, throwing the unused pencil she was holding onto the desk. "Who am I trying to kid?" She jerked open the bottom drawer of her desk, searching for the bottle of aspirin she kept handy.

"Need some water for those?"

Glancing up, Bobbi saw Ralph standing in her doorway. She didn't even bother to conjure up a smile, though, knowing any pretense on her part wouldn't have a chance of getting past him.

"Sure would help," she answered softly, and Ralph disappeared, returning a moment later with a plastic cup of cool bottled water.

"Here you go," he said, handing it to her and watching closely as she downed the two tablets.

Sighing deeply, Bobbi leaned back in her chair and closed her eyes, willing away the pounding in her forehead and the throbbing behind her eyeballs.

"Thanks Ralph," she whispered.

"Sure," he said, eyeing Bobbi's ravished-looking features with a great deal of concern. He pulled out the chair opposite her desk and sat down. "Want to talk about it?" he asked bluntly.

Slowly Bobbi's eyelids opened. "Talk about what?" she answered evasively.

"About the way you look. Terrible."

"I thought you said I never look bad," she said, managing a paltry grin. "You've just hurt my feelings, Ralph."

"Sorry about that, but it's the truth, you know. I realize Mondays aren't the greatest, but you look as though this one's killing you."

Bobbi reached up with one hand to massage her forehead. "That's a fairly accurate description."

Ralph's lips compressed, then he glanced at his watch. "I have a suggestion. Why don't we talk about it over lunch? On me today," he added with an encouraging smile.

Bobbi winced at the thought of even standing up, let alone going to the trouble of braving the afternoon lunch crowd. "Thanks, Ralph, but I just—"

"We'll go to Michel's."

Bobbi looked at him in open surprise. "Michel's? For lunch?"

Ralph grinned broadly and gestured with one hand, palm outward. "Why not? Us working class folk deserve a treat every once in a while."

"I'll second that. But on a Monday? For lunch?"

"The perfect day," he insisted firmly, and Bobbi had to admit that the prospect of going to Michel's for lunch instead of the usual noisy places they frequented was indeed an inviting one. And she *could* do with a bit of nourishment, especially the delicious cuisine the secluded, uncrowded French restaurant had to offer.

"All right, then," she agreed without further consideration, "you're on."

"Great," Ralph said, standing and walking toward the door. "Meet you in the lobby in, say, twenty minutes?"

"Fine," Bobbi agreed, sitting up straight in her chair then, smiling gratefully at him for the timely suggestion. Whatever would she do without good old Ralph?

The atmosphere at Michel's exuded sophistication and money in everything, from the well-prepared and displayed food to the understated atmosphere of quiet elegance. Formally attired waiters moved noiselessly throughout the partitioned dining areas, a background of classical music mingling with the tinkling of silver and china and the subdued voices of patrons.

Bobbi and Ralph dined on crab-stuffed mushroom cap appetizers as they waited for their entrées. Reasoning that it would be prudent to get the subject out in the open from the start, Bobbi launched into a full account of Blain Pearson's sudden appearance in her life that past weekend.

"Whew." Ralph shook his head in astonishment as she finished. "You should have called me, Bobbi. You shouldn't have had to put up with the guy's threats like that." He frowned, his brown eyes peering at her from behind his black-framed glasses. "I must say, it certainly doesn't sound like you, giving in so readily."

Bobbi averted her gaze and sipped her iced tea thoughtfully. It wouldn't do to tell the entire story at that point. She'd best let Ralph believe what he wanted concerning her motives.

"Well, I hope you've seen the last of him," Ralph commented dryly, spearing another mushroom.

Bobbi murmured something as she drank some more of the tea; Blain's possession of her extra key was hardly reassuring as far as that went. An anxious knot curled up within her as she considered what Ralph would think of *that*. But Ralph apparently understood her mumble as a confirmation, for he changed the subject, completely dropping that of Blain Pearson.

Bobbi smiled and feigned interest in the rest of the conversation, yet she was certain Ralph was aware of her preoccupied mood. Ever the gentleman, however, he made no comment, carrying on as though everything were quite normal. Bobbi loved him for his thoughtfulness, and by the time they were ready to leave she was indeed in far greater spirits.

Ralph opened the passenger door of his car, and

Bobbi slid inside, placing her purse on the seat next to her as Ralph went around to the driver's side. She sensed, as always, a comfortableness with him and wasn't at all surprised to find her headache had diminished considerably. Nevertheless she found it difficult to suppress a certain amount of guilt that she'd held back with Ralph on a subject she would have at one time gladly shared with him.

She liked Ralph very much, and although she had insisted on a no-commitment status to the relationship, being particularly careful not to lead him on, it was impossible not to appreciate his obvious caring. Casually she cast a glance at him, mentally assessing his appearance before turning her gaze once more to the scenery outside her window. In all honesty Ralph was not what most women, at least those she knew, would term handsome. On the other hand, he was certainly not unattractive. Of average height and build, he had what some would term an All-American look. His expression, open and receptive, contributed immensely to his likable personality. He was reasonably ambitious and made a steady, dependable income. He was responsible. In short, Bobbi was well aware that she could have done a good deal worse for a devoted admirer.

She smiled and nodded as Ralph asked her something, hoping she'd answered it correctly. Her chest rose and fell as she expelled a silent sigh. So what was she just waiting around for? she asked herself. Why was she still insisting on a wall between the two of them, a wall that once removed would mean a closer, more permanent relationship?

And it *was* about time to start thinking seriously about the permanent relationship she had avoided so assiduously until then. Yet the mere idea of the vicious cycle so many of her friends had been caught up in made her cringe inwardly; marriage, children, then within five to seven years the inevitable divorce. Scramble, then do it all over again. How could they do it; go through all that pain and separation, then throw themselves back into the fire so eagerly? Of course, it was true, a substantial percentage of second marriages were successful and lasting, so one couldn't blame people for at least trying.

But what Bobbi simply couldn't fathom was the rush. Why not wait a few years, get to know oneself better, one's needs and desires, thereby knowing what sort of mate one required? Pragmatism. That's what most people, as far as Bobbi could ascertain, were lacking. Good old-fashioned pragmatism. If anything, she possessed it in abundance. She had been pragmatic enough *not* to marry her first love, whom she had met at college, choosing instead to realize that it was just that—a first love.

Yet time had passed since college, a lot of time. And, curiously, it seemed that the hands of time were speeding up; a week was like a day, a month like six, and on and on. She supposed it was not an original discovery by any means, but nevertheless she was becoming increasingly aware of it. In barely a month she would be twenty-seven. Twenty-seven! Unconsciously she swallowed. She knew that wasn't old, but yet, it seemed so . . . so old! She couldn't help it; there was a sense of urgency gripping her more and more every day, as if now, more than ever, she needed to set her priorities straight and get on with what she had planned for her life.

Ralph was pulling into the parking lot, and Bobbi came back to reality. Her headache hadn't returned, but the tension nagging at her had intensified. Hopefully she could channel it productively and get some of the work done that awaited her.

"Ralph," she said as they walked toward the building, "thanks immensely."

"Strictly my pleasure," Ralph said cheerfully, holding open the glass door as Bobbi preceded him inside.

"Whatever would I do without you to pick me up when I'm so down?" she asked, smiling balefully as they continued toward the elevators.

"That's something you'll never have to find out," Ralph assured her, pressing the Plexiglas button.

Bobbi's smile widened as she stepped into the elevator, thinking again how very, very fortunate she was in simply knowing him.

The telephone was ringing as she walked inside the apartment that evening. Hurriedly Bobbi let herself in, a sharp prickle of anticipation causing her breathing to accelerate slightly as she picked up the receiver and answered.

"Well, finally," Mary Beth said as soon as Bobbi's hello was out.

"Oh, hi, Mary Beth," Bobbi greeted her friend. "When did you get in?" Weariness washed over her suddenly, and she slipped her shoulder bag onto the couch and plopped down, kicking off her shoes and wiggling her toes.

"Late last night, like I said I would." Mary Beth hesitated, then went on. "And somehow I can tell you couldn't really care less about the subject of my trip."

"That's not true," Bobbi objected halfheartedly. "I want to hear all about your weekend rendezvous."

"Huh! You'll have to sound a little more enthusiastic than that to convince me. But it doesn't matter. I'm gonna tell you all about it anyway."

Bobbi sighed deeply and closed her eyes, thinking she may as well relax for the rest of the conversation. A mere few days ago she would have listened with genuine interest to Mary Beth's relating of her weekend with Rick, the current love in her life. She'd never been to New Orleans herself, and Mary Beth was so entertaining that anything she described had a way of becoming a vicarious enjoyment for Bobbi. Today, however, it was an effort to even pay attention, let alone pretend enthusiasm.

"Sounds like you had a fantastic time," she commented at the end of Mary Beth's story.

"I *really* did. And Rick is *so* gorgeous." Mary Beth sighed dramatically.

"When will you see him again?"

"Mmmm. I'm not sure. He's supposed to call at the end of the week and let me know when he'll be back in town."

Rick Parker's position as sales representative for a major medical supply company demanded that he travel a great deal, a fact that hardly bothered Mary Beth in the least. She and Bobbi had discussed that particular state of affairs on numerous occasions and had as yet to see eye to eye on the matter. Bobbi maintained that Mary Beth was crazy to continue a relationship that was part-time at best, but Mary Beth, on the other hand, had claimed that at least it was never, ever lacking in romance. Distance, in their case, had made the heart—and passion—grow imminently stronger.

"So what did you do this weekend?" Mary Beth switched the subject.

Bobbi hesitated, momentarily dumbstruck and uncharacteristically unsure of her answer.

"Well?" Mary Beth persisted, and by the tone of her voice Bobbi had no doubt she wouldn't get away withholding any information her friend thought was absolutely vital to their relationship, which excluded very little of even the most intimate details of one another's lives.

"Well...it was unusual."

"What is that supposed to mean?"

Bobbi groaned. "Look, Mary Beth, it's not something I can just tell you about over the phone."

"Why not?" Mary Beth demanded.

"Because it will take too long."

"Okay. But give me a hint at least. What's his name?"

Again Bobbi hesitated.

"I knew it." Mary Beth pounced on the silent affirmation, then added derisively, "Not Ralph I hope."

"No," Bobbi replied tiredly. "Not Ralph."

"This is ridiculous, Bobbi. What are we doing? Playing some kind of game?"

Bobbi sat up and lifted a hand to unpin her hair, which she had worn in a twisted coil at her nape. It was a no-win situation with Mary Beth, she knew that. Once she let the cat out of the bag, so to speak, there was no stopping the woman from extracting every last detail out of her. If she tried to keep things to herself, it would just be a matter of time anyway.

"All right," she relented finally. "Blain Pearson was here this weekend."

"What!" Mary Beth was downright incredulous. "You don't mean *the* Blain Pearson—the basketball player you've been tracking down all this time?"

"One and the same," Bobbi admitted reluctantly.

"Well, if that doesn't beat everything! What was he doing at *your* place? I don't—"

"He stayed here. For the entire weekend."

"Come on! I don't believe you."

"You might as well. I'm not lying. He spent the weekend here in my apartment." Oddly the words sent a certain sensation of excitement through her veins, a thrill that was every bit as surprising as her news was to Mary Beth.

For once Mary Beth was speechless. Bobbi could almost visualize her shaking her head, her brown eyes bugging out disbelievingly.

"Have you eaten supper?" Mary Beth asked suddenly.

"No . . . but why—"

"Then just slip into something comfortable, and I'll be there in, say, half an hour."

"But—"

"Pizza sound good?"

"Sure, but, Mary Beth, I—"

"Great. I'll just run down to Pizza Inn and pick one up for us. Do you have anything to drink?"

"No." After Blain, she had virtually nothing left in her apartment. She'd *have* to go shopping, but just the thought of it made her want to crawl into bed and go to sleep.

"I'll bring something, then. See you in a little while."

Bobbi's good-bye met the steady whine of the dial tone. Resignedly she hung up the telephone and stared straight ahead. She had absolutely no idea how she was going to make it through an evening of discussing Blain Pearson all over again, especially with the insatiably curious Mary Beth.

But then, she admitted truthfully, her pantry and refrigerator *were* almost empty, and the pizza did sound awfully good.

Chapter Nine

Mary Beth made herself right at home as usual, whisking about Bobbi's kitchen, setting out plates and utensils, filling the glasses with ice. Bobbi turned on the television to a national news program, adjusting the portable stand so they could watch and eat at the same time, and, hopefully, talk less.

Mary Beth, however, had other intentions. She ignored the international crises and economic woes depicted on the screen, launching directly into the subject that had drawn her over there in the first place. "You know," she stated thoughtfully, "you look weird." She scooped up a slice of pizza and set it on Bobbi's plate.

"Why, thanks," Bobbi replied with mock sincerity. "You're a great friend, you know. You come over and bring me supper—my favorite pizza—then proceed to tell me how terrible I look."

"I didn't say terrible," Mary Beth corrected her. "I said weird."

Bobbi pulled out a chair and sat down, reached for her glass of Coke, and took a sip. "Oh, that's much better. I don't look terrible. Just weird."

"I mean it," Mary Beth said matter-of-factly, tearing off a piece of crust and popping it into her mouth. "You look different. But a different 'different.' You know, just...kind of weird."

Bobbi had to chuckle at Mary Beth's choice of words.

"I'm serious," Mary Beth added between bites. "I could tell the minute I walked through the door that whatever happened this past weekend really affected you."

"I guess you could say that," Bobbi admitted quietly. She picked up her own piece of pizza and bit into the thin, crusty pastry liberally spread with a mixture of cheese, mushrooms, and onions atop a spicy tomato base. It was delicious, but any hope that Mary Beth would focus her attention on the meal was quickly squelched.

"Well, let's hear it," she said between bites.

"I don't suppose there's any way I can get out of it," Bobbi said on a questioning note.

"I don't know why you'd want to and, anyway, no, you can't."

Reluctantly Bobbi revealed the events of the previous weekend. After having related the story once already that day to Ralph, the telling of it was somewhat easier, especially since the listener was her best girl friend. She felt free to include details she'd omitted with Ralph, and Mary Beth's overall perception of the story was totally different. Where Ralph had expressed worry and concern, Mary Beth hooted with laughter at some of the things Bobbi told her.

"I love it." Mary Beth chuckled in her contagiously warm, throaty laugh. "I can just see him with *your* robe on. How far did it reach? His belly button?"

Bobbi, who had begun to smile, now laughed at the recollection herself. It was true; if nothing else, the weekend sure made a hell of a story. Now, what did that mean? If nothing else? Of course there would be nothing else.

Mary Beth prided herself on what she considered a highly developed sense of intuition. In spite of her amusement she recognized the fact that humor was not the overriding matter of importance in the situation involving Blain Pearson. When she'd commented that Bobbi looked weird, she'd meant it; there was a quality to her friend's green eyes that Mary Beth had never observed. As far as she was concerned, there could only be one reason for such a change in a woman's eyes: a man. After all the time of watching the cool, sophisticated Bobbi remain steadfastly uninvolved, she now had the sweet pleasure of knowing that at last she too had been bitten.

Bobbi had more or less wound up her story, and Mary Beth appeared to be studying her, the intensity of her perusal making Bobbi shift uncomfortably in her chair.

"Mary Beth, if you keep staring at me that way, I really am gonna feel weird."

Mary Beth lifted a forefinger and pointed it at Bobbi; the accusing lawyer badgering the helpless witness on the stand.

"*You* are in love," she stated categorically. She

lifted her arms to cross over her chest, her eyes glued to Bobbi's face, which had suddenly deepened to tomato red as she flushed uncomfortably.

"That's the most ridiculous thing I think I've ever heard you say," Bobbi sputtered, almost choking on the last of her pizza.

Mary Beth shook her head from side to side slowly. "I've been known to make a mistake or two before, but I feel pretty positive about this one."

Bobbi rolled her eyes heavenward. "Please, spare me this time, Mary Beth. It's been a long day, and I'm not up to a discussion of your extraordinary intuitive powers."

"But this time they really are coming to me. Really strong." Mary Beth jumped up, warming excitedly to her subject. She walked into the living room and turned off the television. "I'm serious about this, Bobbi. I can...I don't know, *sense* something. I knew it when I walked in and first saw you. Like I said. You looked weird."

Bobbi stood and closed the cardboard lid to the leftover pizza. She picked up the two plates and walked into the kitchen. "I'm going to have to listen to this," she muttered to herself. She opened the refrigerator door. "Do you want any more Coke?"

"Yeah." Mary Beth followed her into the kitchen and put her empty glass down on the counter. As Bobbi filled it and then set about cleaning up, Mary Beth leaned against the counter, watching as Bobbi walked back and forth across the small kitchen. "There is a reason for Blain Pearson just moving in on you like that this weekend. More than your mistakenly repossessing his car."

"I had lunch with Ralph today," Bobbi inserted, in a futile attempt to change the subject.

"What?"

"I said I had lunch with Ralph today."

Mary Beth barely acknowledged that piece of information as she went on in the same vein. "I think someone like him would be good for you."

"He is," Bobbi agreed. "Ralph's a tremendous man. A tremendous *person,* for that matter. I—"

"I'm talking about Blain," Mary Beth interrupted, frowning.

Bobbi faced her friend, placing one hand on her hip as she demanded, "You've never even met the man. Don't you think that's being just a *little* presumptuous to assume he's good for me?"

"I don't have to meet him," Mary Beth insisted. "I've read about him."

"Sports articles. About how he can dribble a ball!"

Mary Beth waved a dismissing hand. "You told me about him when you were doing all that research, trying to find him and his car."

"All of it negative, too."

"But he was innocent, wasn't he? It was your mistake."

"AMAC's mistake," Bobbi objected. "A computer, or computer programmer, mistake, not mine."

"Just the same, he was innocent."

Bobbi shrugged. "Well, so what?"

Suddenly Mary Beth's face took on a pleading, dramatic expression. "You *need* a man like Blain Pearson, Bobbi. Someone to wake you up. Introduce you to the real world."

"Oh, come on, Mary Beth," Bobbi interjected derisively. "I wasn't born yesterday. I've been in love before, I'm not exactly a hermit as far as other relationships go, and I'm very pleased with my life the way it is."

"Are you?" Mary Beth's eyes narrowed skeptically.

"Of course," Bobbi insisted, but she turned her back to her overly perceptive friend and gave her full attention to the dishes in the sink. She wasn't about to let Mary Beth capitalize on the abrupt sensation the question had caused to flit around inside her. The conversation was getting entirely out of hand. She didn't mind sharing her personal feelings on most subjects with Mary Beth, but her friend was about to overstep her bounds.

Mary Beth would not have made claim to her intuitive powers had she not been so convinced of their validity; and she was as convinced of them as ever as she wisely eased the tense atmosphere by walking into the living room and switching on the television. She had every intention of proving her point, but the subject could wait for a while. She plopped down on the couch and set her Coke down atop a coaster on the coffee table.

"Anything special you wanted to watch?" she asked, glancing at Bobbi through the kitchen-living room bar window.

Bobbi shook her head as she ran water over the dishes before placing them in the dishwasher.

Mary Beth sighed and pressed the sound button on the remote control to the lowest setting. "I think I'm going to quit my job."

"When?" Bobbi challenged.

"As soon as possible. Either that or strangle Myrtle Hankower."

Bobbi relaxed somewhat and chuckled lightly. "If you ever get around to doing either, I'll faint. What's happened now?"

Mary Beth took a healthy swig of her Coke and set it back down heavily. "You're not gonna believe it.... That woman is determined to make my life miserable. Today Mr. Woodson asked me to take care of..."

Bobbi listened obligingly to Mary Beth's recounting of how unjust life was in that she, of all the secretaries in her office, had to put up with the Wicked Witch of the East, Myrtle Hankower. Approximately once a month Bobbi's sympathetic ear was called upon to listen to the woes and frustrations of Mary Beth's work life, most of it involving good old Myrtle. But Bobbi was grateful for the timely change of subject; further mention of Blain Pearson was never made the rest of the evening.

Mary Beth left for her own apartment shortly before ten o'clock, and after locking up, Bobbi walked into her bedroom, undressed, and practically collapsed onto the bed. She'd just closed her eyes and was starting to drift off when suddenly they popped open. She'd forgotten to set the alarm. Exhaustedly she switched on the bedside lamp and reached over to set the alarm. Simultaneously the telephone rang, and Bobbi frowned as she wondered who would be calling at that time of night. As usual, her first thought in such a situation was that she hoped it wasn't an emergency involving anyone in her family or among her friends.

Blain's voice, therefore, caught her totally off guard. "Bobbi? Did I wake you up?"

"Blain? Is that you?" In one fell swoop her exhaustion was put on hold and Bobbi felt more alert than she'd been all day long. Her heart thumped ridiculously and she found it surprisingly difficult to steady her wavering voice.

"Yes. Can't you hear me very well?"

"No...no, I can hear you fine. You sound far away, but I can understand you." She hesitated. "Where *are* you?"

"Just got into Cleveland this afternoon. We'll be here a couple of days, then we fly down to Houston."

"Oh." It was absolutely ridiculous, she thought, angry with herself for letting him get to her like this.

Blain was saying, "Listen, I'll get to the point of this call. Are you going to be busy this weekend?"

"N-no, not really," Bobbi answered, taken aback by the question. She was at once unsure of the prudence of her answer; she probably should have said just the opposite.

"Then I have a suggestion. Why don't you fly down to Dallas and meet me for the weekend?"

A warm tingling sensation spread quickly up Bobbi's neck and face, and her eyes darted about the room as she frantically pondered the unexpected request. The implications hit her full force, yet she would have been lying to deny the anticipation they generated. And what was that emotion doing, hovering around so precariously, threatening to spew forth in an affirmative reply? Yet, strangely, she could only summon an evasive answer, instead of the flat refusal he deserved. The nerve of the man!

"Well, actually, I—there might be some work I have to take care of this weekend. Things are really getting busy, and—"

"You don't have to give me an answer tonight," Blain inserted smoothly. "Tell you what. I'll give you a couple of days to get things squared away, and then I'll give you a call."

Bobbi suddenly could say nothing.

"I'll let you go, then," Blain said. "And, Bobbi..."

"Yes?"

"You're not going to slip into any old bad habits since I've left, are you...like skipping breakfast?"

Bobbi laughed lightly. "Why, of course not," she replied with feigned enthusiasm. "I don't want to be lacking any vital morning energy, do I?"

"Good girl." Blain laughed, and Bobbi couldn't help but react to the rich, warm sound of his voice. A vibrant tingling shivered down the length of her spinal cord, as if he had magically made physical contact with her. Almost shuddering, she managed, "Good night, Blain."

"Good night. Sleep tight."

The long-distance static ceased as the line clicked off, and Bobbi replaced the receiver in its cradle gently, staring at it for a long moment before lying back and resting her head upon the pillow. Gradually her heart rate returned to normal, but her mind whirled with a riot of confusion and ever-increasing temptation. Sleep, which had been mere seconds away only a few minutes earlier, would be erratic and troubled at best.

The next few days of work seemed to race by. Bobbi dug into the piles of data awaiting her attention with an intensity that bordered on mania. There were two reasons for it: determination not to let thoughts of Blain affect her so much that she couldn't function in her normal capacity, and a desperate effort to get him out of her mind for at least a few hours a day. As for the former, she couldn't remember a time when she had worked as hard or productively, the effect, fortunately, immensely rewarding in helping her achieve the latter.

Ralph, as it turned out, complicated the matter of what to do about the forthcoming weekend. On Tuesday he asked Bobbi if he might have a rain check the next Saturday for their broken date the past weekend. As she had done with Blain, Bobbi stalled, saying she would think about it and let him know in a day or two. She was shocked and more than a little angry with herself. What was wrong with her? Of course she should go out with Ralph!

Her brain, as usual of late, was commanding one thing; her heart, unfortunately, was in definite discord. For an ordinary nine-to-five person the thought of dropping everything and flying down to Dallas for the weekend was the most refreshing suggestion she'd come across in a very long time. Bobbi hadn't had a good excuse to take time off for far too long, but confusion reigned within her.

On the one hand, she was sorely tempted to simply throw caution to the wind and forget about what was reasonable and wise, to forget about her long-range intentions for once and to let herself go and have a little fun. In truth, her attraction toward Blain was undeniable, something she could no longer ignore, and perhaps it would subside if she just got it out of her system.

On the other hand, the idea of responding to his beck and call like some eager jock groupie struck her as tastelessly unappealing. She had to admit that she was surprised in more than one way at his calling and making the offer; he'd seemed on Sunday to have forgotten completely what had passed between them the night before. Perhaps he reasoned that having her on his own territory would be more to his advantage. If so, he'd sure made his move to try out the possibility quickly enough!

In spite of the negative connotations of such possible calculations on his part, though, Bobbi simply could not ignore her own needs, her own response to his timely request. Of course, Mary Beth's assertion that she was in love was absolutely absurd. She was very much attracted to Blain...as were hundreds of other women, no doubt.

Ralph lessened the dilemma for Bobbi on Thursday morning. He went to visit her at her office for a few minutes. He was only working half a day, as he had received a call from his father that his mother was being hospitalized for emergency surgery. He'd promised to fly down to Ocala, where they lived, to be with them both. He seemed to be taking the situation in stride, and Bobbi could only wish him well and offer her prayers for his mother's sake.

That evening Mary Beth called almost as soon as Bobbi walked in the door to her apartment.

"Hey, what's up?" her friend greeted her cheerfully.

"Same as always. Piles of work; no let up. What about you?"

"Lots. Rick's gonna be here this weekend. He's getting in tomorrow night."

"That sounds like fun."

"You bet. What I was calling about was to find out if you'd like to get together with us on Saturday. Invite old what's his name...Ralph."

Bobbi sighed. "He's not old, Mary Beth. And, anyway, he left today for Florida. His mother's having an operation."

"Oh. Well, you can join us alone. Or maybe with one of Rick's salesman friends or something."

"Spare me the something," Bobbi said dryly.

"I can't guarantee Robert Redford, but I can promise you'll have fun. Rick is the greatest. I'm dying for you to meet him, Bobbi."

Bobbi smiled. All of Mary Beth's loves were the greatest. "Uh, I don't know. Maybe."

"What do you mean maybe?" Mary Beth pressed. "Do you have another date or something?"

Bobbi wasn't about to get into *that* with her overly curious friend. She was going to make up her own mind, with no interference whatsoever. "I'll probably have a lot of work to catch up on this weekend,"

Bobbi fibbed, knowing the ruse was a little too transparent. Mary Beth could usually see through the holes in her fabrications, but fortunately she let it drop then, undoubtedly due to her preoccupation with Rick at that moment.

"Well, let me know" was all she replied. "Listen, I'm driving out to Tyson's to shop. I need to spiff up my wardrobe before Rick gets here. You want to come along?"

"Thanks, but not tonight," Bobbi declined. "I'm going to hop into the sack early." And not sleep a wink, she thought, until Blain called. What if he didn't?

"Okay. Give me a call tomorrow and let me know if you want to go out with us Saturday."

"All right. Good-bye."

"Bye."

She was just stepping out of the tub a couple of hours later when the telephone rang. Swathing herself in a terry towel, she hurried into the bedroom and picked up the receiver, droplets of moisture from her wet hair trickling down her back.

"Hello?"

"Bobbi? It's me, Blain."

Once again the same sense of heated excitement welled up inside her. "Hi. Are you still in Cleveland? Or Houston?" It was impossible to keep up with his city-hopping schedule.

"Houston. I leave tomorrow for Dallas. How's your work coming along? Can you join me?"

He didn't waste a second getting straight to the

point, Bobbi reflected. Until that moment she had still
not made up her mind about what she was going to
do. She *had* been putting in diligent hours that week,
as a result having accomplished so much, there was
virtually nothing left for tomorrow, let alone the
weekend. Ralph wouldn't be there, and the last thing
she wanted to do was horn in on Mary Beth's romantic scene. Also, she loathed being set up with strangers, even if it was by her best friend.

"Yes," she answered quietly, "I can join you."
Was she really saying that?

"Great," Blain said enthusiastically. "Just in case
you did agree, I made reservations for you on Eastern
Airlines, leaving from Dulles. I've arranged to arrive
a little before you on National. That way we can meet
in the airport."

Bobbi was stunned that he had already laid that
much groundwork. He'd obviously felt fairly sure of
his conquest, and she could hardly object then.

"Which flight is it?" she asked.

Blain gave her the information, which she scribbled
down on the back of an envelope lying on the night-
stand.

"Do you have any idea how much the ticket is?"
she asked, embarrassed at having to ask. *He* might be
able to flit all over the country without a care as to the
cost, but she was not exactly in first-class status.

"Don't worry about that. It's been taken care of."

Bobbi groped for some sort of reply. She'd had no
idea he would actually be *paying* her way.

"Did you write all that down?"

"Yes...yes, I have it."

"Well," Blain said lightheartedly, "I'll see you tomorrow night, then."

"I guess so," Bobbi replied, swallowing deeply.

"Good night, then."

"Good night."

Slowly Bobbi inhaled a long breath. Rather shakily, she expelled it. God, what in the world had she just gotten herself into?

Chapter Ten

The Dallas-Ft. Worth airport was bustling with throngs of people, either passengers waiting to board departing airplanes or those greeting passengers of arriving ones. Bobbi stood just outside the portable corridor, shifting her tote bag on one arm and her shoulder-strap purse on the other. Unlike Virginia, Dallas was warm that time of year, and in spite of the air conditioning, Bobbi felt uncomfortable with the tweed jacket she'd decided to take along. The great numbers of people crowding the lounge created a heat that worked against the cooling effects.

Bobbi shifted nervously from one foot to the other, wishing she could find some place to set her things down and take off the jacket, yet not wanting to go to all that trouble. Her green eyes rounded as she scanned the crowd in search of Blain. He'd said he'd meet her there, but what if his own flight was late? She hated the thought of standing around not knowing where to go or what to do. Well, if worse came to worst, she would— Suddenly she saw him, his dark-auburn head appearing above the crowded lounge as he worked his way toward her.

Bobbi could have sworn that the crowd parted—Moses dividing the waves of the Red Sea—his commanding height placing him in the company of the gods and sainted as far as most were concerned. As before, when they had gone shopping together at Tyson's Mall, certain people stared at them in open curiosity as Blain walked up to her and took her tote bag, slinging it across his own shoulder.

"Hi," Bobbi greeted him. How trite and incongruous the monosyllabic greeting was with the physical reaction of just seeing him again. It was absolutely ridiculous the way the man got to her. He was staring down at her with hooded azure eyes, and Bobbi felt she would melt beneath the probing, almost hungry perusal. She swallowed unconsciously and opened her mouth to say something, but Blain spoke at the same time.

Laughing lightly, though still uncomfortable, Bobbi said, "Go ahead."

Blain's mouth broadened into a warm, sexy smile, and again Bobbi's heart began to somersault. "I said, hello there, pip-squeak. How was your flight?"

Bobbi lifted a hand and tilted it back and forth. "So-so. Couple of rough spots here and there."

"Well, you're here. That's all that matters now." Blain took one of her hands, then began leading her through the crowd, which parted as automatically as before. Bobbi couldn't avoid intercepting some of the looks of recognition. But any fear that Blain would be

accosted again by an army of admiring fans was
quickly dispelled as he led her quickly down the connecting corridor. It was all Bobbi's much shorter legs
could do to keep up with him.

"So how was your flight?" she asked breathlessly.

"Smooth as a baby's bottom."

Bobbi laughed, the first indication, and a welcome
one, that she was beginning to relax.

The two of them chatted lightly as they waited in
the baggage terminal and then stood in line at the car-
leasing counter. Blain was as much at ease as if he did
this sort of thing on a regular basis, which, of course,
he did, Bobbi reminded herself. The excitement she
felt from simply traveling all that way for only a
couple of days was old hat to him. The likelihood
crossed her mind also that meeting girl friends at the
airport for a weekend rendezvous was not an unfamiliar situation to him either.

Blain exited the rental car off Stemmons Freeway and
began decelerating the car. Bobbi fairly gaped as she
stared to her right at the incredibly imposing structure
looming just ahead of them. "*What* is that?" she
asked in amazement.

Blain grinned. "That's where we're staying. The
Anatole."

Dumbstruck, Bobbi stared at the monolithic structure. Without doubt it was the most imposing building
she had ever laid eyes upon. The classic base of the
twenty-five-story building contrasted sharply with a
trio of gigantic clear-span glass pyramid roofs appearing to float above the mass.

"*That* is a hotel?" she asked incredulously. Inset along the front of the hotel were five massive sculptures, all brick and bearing ancient Egyptian themes. The effect of the enormous twenty-foot-high mosaic panels was overwhelming, yet somehow especially fitting for the architectural design of the hotel.

"Actually, it's more than that," Blain informed her. "It's a hotel, conference center, and health club facility rolled into one." He stepped out of the car and handed the keys to a crisply uniformed valet, then went around to help Bobbi out. A bellman was instantly at their sides and within seconds had gathered their luggage onto a cart and was taking it inside.

Bobbi was all too aware of the provincial picture she must have made, staring like some country bumpkin, but it couldn't be helped; she was simply awestruck.

As they entered the huge marble-floored lobby Blain pulled her close to him, and his fresh male scent teased her senses, making her lean in closer to him. Why, she wondered vaguely, did something that was obviously so wrong for her feel so absolutely right? But the warning message flitted out of her brain as rapidly as it had appeared; the decision had been made, and she *would* carry it through. Whatever doubts and regrets that might eventually plague her were put on hold, to be considered next week.

The interior of the Anatole was even more imposing than its exterior, Bobbi discovered quickly. Blain approached the registration desk, and she wandered further into the mainstream of the lobby, her head instinctively bending backward as she took in the sheer enormity of it all. There was a certain energy, pulsating and excitingly elegant, exuding from the vast interior, housed beneath the triad of six-story glass pyramids. Uniquely linked dual atria unveiled a virtual landscape of international cities within a city. They were nearer Atria II, and Bobbi gazed in disbelief at the stories-high colorful batiks streaming from the skylights.

Bobbi walked back to where Blain waited at the registration desk. "How old is this place?" she asked quietly.

"About three or four years, I believe," Blain answered.

"May I help you?" the clerk was asking him.

"Reservations for Pearson. Blain Pearson." While the information was being brought up on the computer terminal Blain glanced down at Bobbi, her eyes glittering as though mesmerized by it all.

"I take it you like it," he said, grinning.

"It's fantastic," Bobbi enthused. She turned and frowned up at him. "But was this necessary? I mean, we could have stayed at some place...less ritzy, you know."

Blain shrugged. "Only the best," he said lightly, brushing the crook of his forefinger across the tip of her nose. Blushing furiously, Bobbi turned and looked away, amazed at the intensity of her reaction to such an inconsequential gesture.

On the ride up to their room, or more properly termed, suite, Blain informed Bobbi that they'd actually seen only a portion of the hotel. Since they would be dining in one of the six restaurants housed within the monstrous complex, they could do a more thorough investigation of the place at that time.

The bellman set their luggage down in the sitting area of the sumptuously decorated suite, and Blain tipped him generously. Bobbi waited nervously, not knowing exactly what to do next. She'd never stayed in a place so plush, so... intimate. She was a big girl, totally aware of what she had gotten herself into, but even so an army of butterflies staged a return assault as she watched Blain closing the door and latching it.

Blain, however, obviously suffered no such pangs. He moved about confidently, much the same as he had at her apartment, his sheer physical presence making the room seem a part of him. "Go on and put your purse down," he suggested, turning off the overhead light and switching on one of the lamps in the bedroom. It cast a mellow glow about the generously proportioned suite. Bobbi set her purse down on the couch and took a few steps across the thick brown carpeting into the bedroom.

"Come here," Blain said. "I want to show you something."

As she walked into the bedroom her gaze appreciatively took in the heavy oak furnishings and the framed art reproductions along the walls that lent a distinctive European flair. Just outside the door apparently leading into the bathroom was a travertine vanity and a mirrored makeup area, directly across from a full-length mirrored wardrobe door. It was the king-size bed, though, that seemed, at least to Bobbi, to dominate the entire room. Forcing her eyes to look elsewhere, she swallowed spasmodically, shoving her hands inside the front pockets of her linen skirt and feigning interest in the other amenities of the spacious room.

Blain was standing at the wall-length window and was pulling back the draperies. He turned his head and beckoned to her. "Come here," he said softly.

Bobbi inhaled deeply and walked over to where he stood beside the window, her nervousness temporarily diverted by the magnificent picture below of the downtown Dallas skyline. Nighttime had erased the scars and inconsistencies, a galaxy of lights, like shimmering rhinestones, punctuating its concealing cloak of black velvet. They seemed to be suspended in the midst of it all, and the sense of abandonment Bobbi had experienced earlier was suddenly intensified.

"It's really beautiful, isn't it?" Bobbi commented softly.

"Nighttime always makes a city look better," Blain said, casually slipping his arm around Bobbi's shoulders, drawing her to his side. As before, Bobbi experienced a sense of the rightness of their togetherness, and when he turned to place both arms around her, it felt like the most natural thing in the world.

She felt a shudder traverse the length of Blain's body as he bent his head and gathered her to him. Bobbi raised up on tiptoes to receive Blain's kiss, his lips full and hot, like molten lava, mere symptoms of the explosive fires he held within. There was no way she could have held back her own response; she wanted what was happening, needed it with an intensity that shocked her. Instinctively her hands kneaded Blain's lean muscular back in long sensuous strokes.

Blain's own hands were not unoccupied; tenderly his fingers threaded through the curtain of her hair, exploring the sensitive flesh behind her ears. As their mouths opened, exploring and tasting the heady warmth within, at first tentatively, then hungrily, Blain dropped one hand to her shoulder, stroking and gently squeezing it before moving his hand further to cup her breast within its palm. Deftly he moved his other hand, his thumb lazily tracing the labyrinthine contours of her ear.

Bobbi moaned softly and shuddered; she felt as if an electric current had ignited her nervous system. The pressure of his hard, potent form against hers thrust excitement to a fever pitch. Reasoning thoughts threaded their way through the whirlwind of emotions in her mind, lending her a vestige of control over her runaway passions.

"Blain?" She muttered his name almost incoherently between their lips.

"Hmmm?"

"I...I'm hungry." She couldn't have eaten a thing if it was forced upon her right then, but she had to do *something*. Her behavior had certainly not been her intention, in spite of what he might think to the contrary; she wasn't exactly in the habit of conducting weekend trysts, let alone beginning them immediately by making love.

Blain groaned reluctantly, but only partially released her. "You are?" he asked obligingly.

"Uh-huh." She reached up and removed his hand from the side of her neck. "I think I should unpack and freshen up before we go down."

Blain stared at her hungrily for an anguished moment, then dropped both hands, shoving them into the pockets of his slacks.

"Right," he said, turning to gaze once more at the downtown Dallas skyline.

Bobbi returned to the sitting room and, after laying her suitcase flat, began to unpack. Soft violin strains drifted through the suite as Blain switched on the stereo system to a classical station. Gradually Bobbi's breathing returned to normal and, after finally unpacking the last of her clothes, she escaped into the bathroom for a few moments of sorely needed privacy.

The wall-length mirror above the marble vanity was surrounded with makeup lights, and Bobbi peered at her image almost shyly. Indeed it was a good thing that only the mirror was seeing her at that moment. Her fair complexion was tinged with an all-too-revealing crimson stain. She was unused to seeing herself in such a vulnerable light, and impulsively she swept back the locks of hair that were still tangled from Blain's fingers. She turned on the taps, unwrapped a bar of scented hotel soap, and began to lather her face vigorously.

When she emerged ten minutes later, there was a renewed freshness to her face and her hair had resumed its brushed, smooth look. Blain indicated that he would like to take his turn in the bathroom, and while he was doing so Bobbi quickly changed out of the skirt and blouse she had traveled in, putting on one of her favorite dresses, a dark blue silk shift belted with a sash of silky forest green. She chose a simple strand of gold from which dangled a diamond-encrusted heart, definitely her most expensive piece of jewelry besides the earrings she wore. A pair of twisted gold knots, they were dainty, yet large enough to catch one's attention whenever her hair happened to swing back from the sides of her neck.

She had just slid her feet into a pair of ankle-strapped high-heeled sandals when Blain came back into the room. He too looked refreshed, but when he caught his first glimpse of Bobbi, the appreciative gleam in his eyes revealed far more than any complimentary words ever could have.

They stared at one another distractedly for what seemed an eternity. Bobbi rose from the bamboo-printed love seat, crossing the room to the handsomely carved oak triple dresser. She picked up her clutch bag and turned to Blain.

"Ready?"

Blain nodded as he pocketed his wallet and the room key and walked to the door to open it. As he made sure the room was locked while they stood in the carpeted hallway, he asked, "Which restaurant would you like to eat in tonight?"

"What are my choices?" Bobbi asked as they walked toward the elevators.

The dining there, Blain explained, ranged from that served by authentic Chinese, northern Mexican, and haute cuisine French restaurants to a sixty-six-foot high kiosk called Mirage, which served a variety of sandwiches and snacks and exotic ice creams. In addition, there was a coffee house, a luxurious cocktail lounge, and a disco club with a bar. Bobbi declared that Chinese sounded good that night, so the two of them strolled through the luxurious surroundings as they made their way to the Plum Blossom restaurant.

There, as in the rest of the hotel, the decor was plush and cleverly decorated. A seven-foot high Buddha nestled alongside seven large Chinese scrolls, various sculptures, and a grand black-lacquered Chinese console inlaid with mother-of-pearl. The meal was delicious and the conversation relaxed, most of it involving what each had been doing over the past week.

Afterward, as they sat sipping the rest of the wine, Bobbi asked, "Blain, when is your game this weekend?"

"There isn't one," he answered, and Bobbi frowned at the unexpected answer. "It's Monday night."

"Then what—" The idea that he had simply asked her to join him for a weekend in Dallas for no other reason than for the two of them to be together somehow struck her as rather unlikely.

"I have a meeting scheduled for early Monday morning with my agent."

"Oh." She was curious as to the reason but hesitated to pursue the subject.

As if reading her mind, Blain said, "Terms of my contract, that sort of stuff."

Bobbi nodded and sipped her wine. For some reason—was it the preoccupied expression that drifted momentarily across Blain's face?—she surmised that the "stuff" he was referring to was of an involved nature. She really knew comparatively little about the business aspects of a basketball professional's life and was therefore at a loss to even know what questions to ask, let alone the proper ones.

And besides, she was of a much too agitated frame of mind to think very long about a matter that had little, if anything, to do with her.

Chapter Eleven

Bobbi set her purse down on the dresser and fiddled with the zipper in a distracted gesture. The gut-wrenching sensation had expanded to an almost overwhelming nervousness. The soothing effects of the wine had apparently vanished completely, and once again she wrangled with her conflicting emotions. Drinking had never been her forte, but at the moment she could certainly see the merits of a stiff one.

When Blain spoke, Bobbi almost jumped, and she struggled to maintain her composure.

"What did you say?" she asked, trying to sound as at ease as possible.

"I asked if you would like to watch television." Blain picked up a pamphlet that lay atop the television. "We have our choice of regular, cable, and blue."

"Blue?" Bobbi frowned.

"X-rated." Blain smiled and wiggled his eyebrows.

"You know, I think I'd prefer to take a bath right now."

"Sure," Blain said, sliding his jacket off his long arms and hanging it up in the closet. He slipped out of his shoes and padded across the carpet to the bed, plopping down on the end of it and turning on the television set.

Bobbi gathered her things and made for the refuge of the bathroom once again. She drew water into the ample-size tub and squeezed in a little of the delicious-smelling pink bath gelée she'd brought along. Within seconds the room was permeated with a scent that reminded her of home, and instinctively she relaxed a bit. She slid the silk dress carefully over her head and hung it on a hanger on the door hook, taking advantage of the steamy atmosphere to remove some of the wrinkles. Twisting her hair up into a knot, she removed the rest of her clothing and slid into the bathtub, welcoming the hot bubble bath.

Apparently Blain was busy watching a cable movie, and Bobbi's tensed muscles relented as she slid farther down into the foamy retreat. A tiny furrow creased her brow as she pondered that particular descriptive term. Retreat from what? From Blain?

No, that was ridiculous. The evening had been a real pleasure. She couldn't imagine having spent it in more enjoyable company. The more Bobbi got to know him, the more it became apparent that Blain was not at all the uneducated jock she had initially pigeonholed him as being. On the contrary, she found him to be well rounded and intelligent, his thinking in many respects blending with her own.

So, then, what was the problem? The question demanded attention and dutifully Bobbi considered it fully. The answer, she finally admitted, was not at all a mysterious one. The crux of the matter lay in the fact that her many self-assured assertions to Mary Beth that she was just as experienced as any other woman of her day and age had stretched the truth in both respects. It was true, she had dated quite a lot, had had several relationships since she and Bill had broken up in her last year of college. In none of them had the sexual aspect been carried to the extent she had shared with Bill. It had not been an easy feat, she reflected wryly, maintaining her rather odd set of standards all that time, but she'd never regretted it.

What was it about Blain that had persuaded her to abandon her principles, even for just the one time? Certainly no hope of a lasting relationship resulting from a single weekend tryst. That could never happen between the two of them. Despite their increasing attraction for one another on levels other than sexual, the cold, hard fact still remained: their totally dissimilar day-to-day lives could never accommodate anything more involved than what they had at that moment.

Three sharp raps on the door jolted Bobbi out of her reverie.

"Yes?" she called out, fairly choking on the word.

"Just wondering if you'd drowned in there," Blain said. Bobbi could almost see him grinning.

"No. I'll be out in a minute," Bobbi said, pushing her toes against the far end of the tub and sitting up. How long had she been lying there? she wondered. Suddenly she felt embarrassed at what he must be thinking of her obvious stalling.

Blain walked across the room to one of the oak nightstands next to the king-size bed. He withdrew his wallet and loose coins from his pants pocket and placed them on top of it. He manipulated the panel of switches on the headboard, which controlled virtually every electric apparatus in the room. He turned down the television volume to the lowest setting and left only one recessed light in the ceiling on.

He listened to the sounds Bobbi made in the bathroom as he slowly unbuttoned his shirt. Knowing that she was going to walk through that door and over to him in a few minutes produced a tightening in his gut. It seemed almost too good to be true. He'd really never expected that she'd accept his offer to meet him in Dallas, especially after the encounter they'd had at her apartment the second night he'd stayed there. At first he'd been angry and confused; she'd responded with as much need and desire as he had, and he'd been so sure.... When she had pulled away and acted so...so *bitchy,* he'd been angry. Really angry. But when it came right down to it, he'd been angry only with himself. He'd been a damn fool to push his luck so soon.

It didn't take too much intelligence to see that she'd been frightened—just as she was obviously frightened this night. He knew that much. He wouldn't make the same mistake. It was enough that she had come; he wasn't about to spoil it.

A band of light swept across the carpet and one wall of the bedroom as Bobbi opened the bathroom door. The scent of her gelée bath wafted out into the rest of the suite, and Blain sniffed appreciatively.

"Mmmm, you smell great," he said, watching as she walked in and hung up her clothes in the closet.

Bobbi glanced furtively at him and bit her lower lip as she noticed that he'd removed his shirt. Dark brown curls matted his broad tapered chest, narrowing to a V that disappeared into the waistband of his slacks. Nervously she dropped a hanger and bent to retrieve it, feeling increasingly silly and insecure.

Blain's eyes followed her hungrily as she walked back and forth across the room, fussing with the contents of her drawers, placing her shoes in the closet—doing every distracting thing she could think of. She was a vision of delicious contrast. Clad in a light blue nylon teddy, she was simultaneously fragile and sultry; innocent yet provocative. The dampness of the bath had darkened her cinnamon-colored locks, creating wispy curls of the baby hair at her forehead. His hands clenched in agitation, then reached up to unbuckle his belt.

The sound of the leather sliding through the loops of his pants caused Bobbi to stop her pretended rearranging of her dresser drawer and glance over at him. She struggled to keep her expression blank, but the telltale widening of her green eyes did not escape Blain's notice.

"Listen," he said in a diversionary tactic. "Do you like Woody Allen?"

"He's all right," she answered, then returned to her rearranging.

Blain switched channels and turned up the volume. "Good. There's one of his movies I've always liked starting in a few minutes."

Bobbi was grateful for the suggestion. Realizing that she was starting to look ridiculous piddling about the way she was, Bobbi walked around to the opposite side of the bed from where Blain was seated. She lifted the covers casually and slipped inside them, fluffing up the pillows behind her and settling back to watch the screen.

For the amount of distance between them, they could have been in separate beds, but Bobbi was achingly aware of Blain's nearness. Slanting a curious look his way, she discovered that fortunately he was still dressed, albeit only halfway, and his attention seemed captured by the verbal comics of Woody Allen.

Gradually Bobbi relaxed and allowed herself to become absorbed in the movie also. The hour was late, however, very late, and the effects of traveling had taken their toll more than she was aware of. Her reclining position did nothing to help sustain an alertness on her part, and within a short time Bobbi's head lolled as her eyes closed.

Blain looked at her, and a soft grin lifted his lips. She looked so vulnerable... it was all he could do to keep from reaching out and pulling her to him, wrapping her within the protective cradle of his arms. Quietly he got up off the bed and turned off the television. The carpet muffled the sound of his footsteps as he visited the bathroom for a few minutes and then finished undressing, taking care to fold his pants across the back of one chair instead of opening the closet door, which had a slight creak.

As he approached the bed he looked down at

Bobbi's sleeping figure and lifted one small hand, massaging its palm against his chin for a thoughtful moment. Then he turned out the light and slid into his own side of the bed, staring into the darkness for an agonized period before drifting off into a restless slumber.

Blain's eyes opened seconds after his ears distinguished the muffled sounds coming from the other side of the bed. Turning his head, he could make out the outline of Bobbi's form, and it seemed that something—her arm?—was reaching out in a flaying motion.

"Bobbi?" he whispered.

She swung her arm again and moaned, the sound resembling a choked cry.

"Bobbi?" he said, more distinctly this time, then repeated it in a loud voice.

But she was lost in another world—some sort of nightmare. Without further hesitation Blain slid across the width of the bed, reluctant to touch her for fear that he might frighten her even more. But he couldn't bear to see her that way, and automatically his hand reached out to grasp the hand that she'd flung out again.

Surprisingly the movement appeared to quieten her, and Blain was encouraged. "Bobbi?" He spoke quietly, squeezing her tiny hand gently.

She made no answer, and he repeated her name, moving his hand to caress the length of her arm.

"Blain?" she whispered, grasping reality as she became aware of his touch.

"I'm here," he assured her in a quiet tone, moving closer to her, massaging her shoulder as she became more lucid. "Bad dream?"

"Uh-huh," Bobbi admitted, sucking in a deep, shuddering breath.

"What was it about?"

Bobbi frowned. "I—I don't really know. I was really scared, though." She swallowed, remembering the panic that had gripped her subconscious so violently. "Did I wake you up?"

"Yes, but that's okay. Are you all right now?"

"Sure." Immensely better, Bobbi thought to herself, relishing in the comfort of Blain's nearness.

"Good." Slowly, almost carefully, Blain bent his head to rest his lips on Bobbi's warm forehead. He kissed her gently, then placing both hands alongside the smooth column of her neck, lowered his mouth to hers, merely pressing the cool flesh of his lips to hers for a long, restoring moment. Tenderly he nibbled her full, sensuous mouth, gently persuading it to open to his own. As if nature willed her, Bobbi complied, their tongues meeting and tasting and exploring in a gradually building crescendo of mutual want and desire.

Bobbi's hands had lifted of their own accord to caress the nape of his neck, her fingers plying the thick dark-auburn mane in sensuous strokes. Slipping his hands supportively around Bobbi's lower back, Blain pulled her to him, leaving one hand to massage the base of her spine in slow hypnotic circles, the other reaching up to slip the wispy straps from her shoulders. When his hand found what it was searching for, his lips followed in pursuit. At first gently, then more firmly, his moistened lips surrounded the crest of first one, then the other, of her achingly full breasts. Methodically he flicked the tip of his tongue around and across them, quickly bringing them to hardened peaks.

Bobbi moaned softly, and instinctively her hips pressed against his. His nakedness excited her immensely, and she was shaking with anticipation when he pulled back to slide the flimsy garment off her slender hips.

He moved to cover her body with his own, deftly balancing his weight on knees and hands. Bobbi's breathing seemed to be suspended for an infinite time and her heart lurched and pounded at a frightful rate, but Blain hesitated, his voice, when he spoke, a tautly controlled whisper.

"Are you sure?" he asked, then felt as much as saw, in the dim light, her assenting nod.

"I won't hurt you, Bobbi," he whispered as he gently lowered himself onto her. "I promise."

Bobbi's eyes, however, winced with the inevitable pain, but the sounds emanating from her throat were a mixture of passionate impatience as well as initial discomfort. She was quickly overcome by the filling, soaring sensations rocking her body with every syncopated movement of their bodies. The sexual act, which she had for so long denied herself, came naturally and easily, and she was at times surprised at the degree of inventive initiative on her own part.

Blain was pleasantly surprised also, and he lovingly encouraged her, finding his own response climbing to a pinnacle he had rarely, if ever, experienced. He coaxed her and encouraged her, responding with supreme joy as she cried out, the sound muffled as her teeth unconsciously sunk into his shoulder. But the bite was sweet, and his own fulfillment followed in a crashing wave behind the wake of hers.

They lay quietly beside one another, their gradually waning erratic breathing patterns the only sounds for several minutes. Bobbi's eyes, which had been closed, blinked open slowly and she turned to stare at the silhouette of Blain's profile.

At first she thought he was asleep, but slowly his head turned to face her, and after seeing that she was awake, too, he slid an arm beneath her and pulled her to his side. With his other hand he retrieved the covers he had kicked back earlier and covered them both.

Bobbi snuggled within the comfort of his arms and relished the simple nearness of him, finding it easy to slip into a peaceful, undisturbed slumber then.

As Blain nestled his face in the fragrant softness of her hair, he listened to the whisper-soft rhythm of Bobbi's contented breathing. His lips curved upward as he smiled at the memory of the unlikely circumstances that had brought her into his life. It was incredible, yet undeniable; he had never known a woman like her, indeed had never taken the time nor felt the inclination. The women in his life—and there had been many, perhaps too many—had lacked the spunk, the vivacity, the sexiness all rolled into this one tiny lady. Suddenly he found himself thinking how nice it would be to wake up every morning with her beside him. His life, which had become so stale and purposeless of late, seemed even bleaker with the knowledge that he could have her this way on a mere temporary basis.

Unless, the sober thought entered his mind, unless he went through with the plans he'd intended on discussing with his agent that week.

Softly, lovingly—for it was impossible to deny that the emotion he felt toward Bobbi was indeed love— he kissed the crown of her head, then rested his own on the pillow beside her. Soon his eyes closed as he drifted into the most peaceful sleep he had known in a long, long while.

As Blain parked the car Sunday morning in the parking lot of the DFW airport, Bobbi had the distinct sensation of having been there only a few hours earlier. Had she really spent two nights with Blain; two glorious nights of incomparable, fulfilling passion? Friday night had been but a prelude to the rapture they had discovered Saturday, the mere thought of what they had shared and learned and taught one another enough to create a quivering inside her even now.

Saturday had been a silly fun-filled lazy day; she couldn't recall ever having been so relaxed and carefree—at least not for a very long while. On impulse they'd visited Six Flags over Texas in nearby Arlington, and Bobbi had felt like a child, stuffing herself with candy and popcorn and allowing Blain to badger her onto the scariest rides.

It had been an equally wonderful evening, filled

with a passion that exceeded that of the one before. The doubts she had wrestled with before about going there were replaced by an intense regret that the time they'd shared was so short. Never in a million years would Bobbi have imagined that she'd be feeling that way, but her feelings were nevertheless impossible to deny. It felt so right, so natural, being with Blain—sharing his days *and* his nights. And it was obvious he felt some degree of emotional attachment toward her, too.

But the fun times were over; today she was flying back to Virginia, and on Monday she would resume her ordinary day-to-day life. Strange how Blain had affected even *that* part of her life. There was a time, and not in the distant past either, when just the thought of what lay ahead each day at work filled her with eagerness and anticipation that fueled the fires of her ambition; an ambition she'd spent the previous five years feeding, nourishing, with hard work and dedication that had seen her excel further and faster than her co-workers. But—and she hated like hell to admit it—there was something missing. It was hard to tell whether the reason had more to do with the fact that perhaps she really was experiencing a typical burn-out dilemma, as Blain had suggested, or whether it was the man himself who'd focused her thoughts and energies on matters of a more emotional nature. She wasn't in the least sure of the answer, and the subject alone was disturbing enough to the unanticipated sense of vulnerability that was seizing her.

The ticket counter was busy, and Bobbi was glad

they had arrived so early, as they had to stand in line for several minutes before clearing her ticket. Walking along the corridor to the departure gate, Blain held Bobbi's hand firmly in his own. Oddly, though, he said very little, and Bobbi was forced to carry the brunt of the conversation. She hated partings of any sort and babbled on uncharacteristically about what the weather was supposed to be like in Virginia.

Blain waited as she made her seating arrangement, then walked with her to stand beside a narrow window that viewed one runway.

He reached for her hand again and held it between both of his own for a long, contemplative moment as he stared out the window. Bobbi was confused by his silence and the gesture.

Finally he released her hand and pressed his lips together in an odd sort of smile. "Do you think you'll know anything by the end of the week? About the Corvette?"

Bobbi hesitated, momentarily at a loss for words. She hadn't expected him to say anything like that; the subject hadn't come up all weekend and to discuss it now filled her with a peculiar distaste.

"We should hear something, I suppose."

"Then I'll be in touch," he said, his gaze rapidly scanning the crowd, which was just then boarding the aircraft. "You'd better get going."

Bobbi turned her head, then reached up to adjust the strap of her tote bag. "Yes, I guess so."

"Have a good flight."

"Yeah. I will."

"Talk to you later, then." He was waving at her as

she began walking away and determinedly she kept herself from looking back at him. If he wanted to play it cool, then, damn it, she would, too. Give you a call, she thought derisively.

Well, I'm not holding my breath, Blain Pearson.

Chapter Twelve

Mary Beth shook her head of tousled light brown hair and stared at Bobbi in stunned disbelief.

"You can't mean it," she stated, then walked over to Bobbi's refrigerator and opened the door. She frowned as she surveyed the sparse contents. "Don't you have anything to drink?"

"I think there may be a can of lemonade or something in the freezer," Bobbi offered in a weary tone. "Or would you prefer coffee? I was going to make some for myself."

"Yeah, all right," Mary Beth agreed, shutting the refrigerator door and walking back into the dining room. She perched on the edge of a chair, propped her elbows on her knees, and rested her chin on the heel of her hand.

"Now, tell me again what I think I just heard. You actually spent the weekend with Blain Pearson? He actually *paid* for you to fly down to meet him in Dallas?"

Bobbi sighed. "You make it sound as though it were some sort of illicit activity," she said derisively.

"My dear, you completely misunderstood me," Mary Beth interjected dramatically. "I think it's the most *exciting* news you've told me in a long time."

Bobbi raised an eyebrow. "I should have known you'd think that."

"Well, of course!" The automatic coffee machine was almost finished brewing, and Mary Beth got up to help Bobbi carry the mugs and cream and sugar to the table.

Evasively Bobbi inquired, "How was your weekend with Rick?"

"Umm, it was okay. We didn't do much. Rick was pretty worn out, so we just loafed around the apartment."

Bobbi was hoping for a more spirited recounting of Mary Beth's weekend. She'd known, of course, when Mary Beth had invited herself over this evening, that one way or another she'd extract from Bobbi the details of the past weekend, but first she was in dire need of a lift from the coffee to sustain the effort of doing just that.

Miraculously Bobbi had made it through a typical Monday workday, using the same tactics she had before by diving in and practically burying herself in her work. Ralph had still been absent, and one of his assistants had informed her that he wouldn't be back until Wednesday. She hoped his mother was doing all right but couldn't help selfishly thinking how much nicer it would be to have him around just then. Unlike the last time she had left Blain, Ralph wasn't there to lend his comforting presence, and she really missed that.

"I want to hear every last detail," Mary Beth was saying as she stirred her coffee. She held up a forefinger. "But first...the most important detail." She grinned conspiratorially. "How was he in bed?"

Bobbi gaped in obvious embarrassment at her friend. Even though she was used to Mary Beth's bluntness, the question truly took her off guard. "Mary Beth!"

"Oh, come on, Bobbi." The other girl waved a hand dismissively in the air. "I know you couldn't have spent the whole weekend in the same room and not— You did share a room, didn't you?"

Bobbi nodded, and Mary Beth continued, apparently relieved. "Well, then, all I'm asking is that you tell the most important details first." Her small crescent-shaped brown eyes peered at Bobbi and her eyebrows rose expectantly.

Bobbi stalled for a moment longer by lifting her mug to her lips and sipping at the steaming brew.

"Well?" Mary Beth prompted impatiently. "Tell me...how was he in the sack?"

Mary Beth was certainly the one and only friend Bobbi had ever had who could get away with such blatancy concerning such an intimate subject. She knew there was absolutely no harm intended, and Mary Beth's unaffected manner of displaying her abundant curiosity was both disarming and inoffensive.

Bobbi couldn't suppress the tiny smile curling the corners of her mouth. "He was...nice. Very nice." *That* was an understatement if anything was. Saturday night had been a treasure trove of physical discovery.

She and Blain had been insatiable, making love with wildest abandonment, falling asleep for a short while, then awakening to an even greater passionate urge for one another. Bobbi couldn't have imagined a more sensitive, patient lover than Blain. Even now the sheer memory of his naked, sweat-glistening body, wrapped so tightly, so completely against and within her own, evoked a surge of sensuous awakening in the pit of her being.

But the memory was marred by a far more disturbing one—that at the airport. She couldn't fathom Blain's attitude.... Nonchalant would be putting it lightly. His behavior had been so much at odds with his caring closeness of the preceding time they'd spent together. She didn't understand it. Perhaps he'd had other, more important things on his mind...like the game, the meeting with his agent, being together with his teammates. All the other things that excluded her from the rest of his life.

Mary Beth set her mug down on the table with a clank and giggled delightedly. "I *knew* it. I could tell there was something different about you when I walked in."

Bobbi laughed despite the discomforting pang within. "Now, don't you think you're overdoing that intuitive bit? That's the second time in two weeks you've said that."

Mary Beth proceeded to substantiate her powers of perceptiveness and finally coaxed Bobbi into a full recounting of the past weekend.

Later that night as she lay in bed Bobbi thought how surprisingly easy it had been to relate everything.

She had felt a surge of happiness and a measure of the joy and pleasure she had shared with Blain, and it was only concerning their parting scene at the airport that she had skimped over most of the details.

In spite of her own noncommittal attitude toward their weekend rendezvous, Bobbi had still expected Blain to at least make some sort of plans for seeing her again. He seemed to be far more concerned about his damn car... which, of course, was understandable.

She had no doubt that he'd enjoyed the weekend with her, but he had only confirmed her suspicion that it held none of the significance it had held for her. She had suspected from the beginning that she was probably only one in a lineup of on-the-road entertainment he kept on a rotating basis. She supposed he really wasn't to blame; after all, the life-style he led was lonely and probably even boring at times.

But why was she letting it get to her that way? Hadn't she promised herself in the beginning that she would simply regard their time together as a temporary diversion, a once-in-a-lifetime experience that would be quickly forgotten as soon as she settled back into the normal routine of her life?

The problem was, of course, she hadn't stopped thinking about the weekend, or Blain, for one minute since she'd been home. The only time she'd been able to successfully forget about him had been those moments at work when she'd been tied up on the telephone or deeply involved in setting up a particular file. Obviously, though, she couldn't work all the time. There were going to be times, like just then, when she would require something else to get her mind back on the business of carrying on with her life in the manner she had planned to.

The answer was so obvious, it seemed incredible she had overlooked it that long; another person, not just another something, was the way to take her mind off Blain Pearson. Admittedly she had made a serious mistake by letting her emotions become so involved with a man she knew to be all wrong for her—in spite of how right she felt when they were together. But one could correct one's mistakes, couldn't one?

Yes, of course, Bobbi assured herself. She closed her eyes, and Ralph's image flitted before the darkened screen of her lids. Ralph's friendly, interested face, ever expressing his sincere concern for her welfare. When was he due back from Florida? Oh, yes, day after tomorrow. The knowledge was heartening, and gradually, putting further thoughts aside, she drifted off to a dreamless sleep.

Bobbi knocked twice on the doorframe of Ralph's office, a virtual fishbowl of completely glassed-in walls. He glanced up from his telephone conversation and waved at her to walk inside.

She stepped inside the tiny cubicle and glanced around; there was no extra chair, so she leaned against a file cabinet and perused the folder she held in one hand, waiting for Ralph to finish his conversation.

"Well, this is a surprise," Ralph said as he hung up, smiling at Bobbi. "Not very much that brings you to this section of AMAC."

Bobbi smiled back at him. "You did. I wanted to find out how things went in Florida. Is your mother all right?"

"She'll be okay. The exploratory surgery didn't find anything major, but it did reveal some minor problems that may have contributed to her symptoms. She'll be going home by the end of the week, but she'll be off her feet for quite a while."

"Well, I'm glad it wasn't anything more serious."

"So am I."

"Well," Bobbi said, sighing, "I just wanted to welcome you back and see that everything was okay." Was she repeating herself as much as it sounded?

"How was your weekend?" Ralph asked politely.

Bobbi shrugged nonchalantly. "Nothing special," she fibbed. Placing her hand on the doorknob, she said, "How about that rain check I owe you? Would you like to do something about it this weekend?"

For the briefest instant Ralph seemed caught off guard, but Bobbi quickly dismissed as inconsequential the rather uncharacteristic flicker that passed across his features.

"Sure," he agreed, "why not? You won't stand me up this time?"

Bobbi gave a brief laugh and shook her head. "No, I promise. I'd love to take in a movie like you suggested. I haven't seen one in a long while. On a big screen, that is. Cable has almost made me forget what it's like to enjoy movies the old way."

"I know what you mean," Ralph agreed. "I'm tied up today, but let's have lunch tomorrow and we'll firm things up."

"Okay," Bobbi agreed as she opened the door. "See you later."

Bud Stamfeld inhaled the last of his cigarette and crushed it out in the near-full ashtray next to him on the table. "You could be making a big mistake, Blain," he said, bringing his lower lip over his upper one in a contemplative mannerism that Blain had observed many times in the years the two of them had been associated. "A really big one."

Blain met the ruddy-faced, bald-headed man's eyes with a seemingly contemplative gaze. He'd been kicking the matter around in his mind for a long time, and the past weekend with Bobbi had been just what he needed to come to a firm conclusion. He'd been playing professional basketball for ten years and he'd had enough. Enough of the life on the road, enough of the bachelor existence that had been so right for a long time but was becoming stale—very stale.

"I've made up my mind, Bud," he stated. "I've considered all the things you've mentioned, but I really and truly think the time is right for me to retire."

Bud shook his head slowly and tapped the back of his soft-pack of cigarettes on the side of one pudgy hand. "I don't know, Blain. You're at your peak now. I'd hate to see you throw it all away." He extracted a cigarette and lit it, exhaling the smoke through his nostrils. "You're never gonna make that kind of money again." His small gray eyes stared hard at Blain.

"I know that," Blain said quietly. "I'm not hurting financially and I don't ever plan to be."

"You're really serious about that coaching position at Duke?"

Blain nodded. "That one and another. I still have to check them out more carefully, but it's something I'd enjoy doing, Bud."

Stamfeld inhaled deeply and let the smoke out of one side of his mouth. "I'd never figured you for this kind of change, but you do sound as though you've convinced yourself of it." The round gray eyes narrowed as he added, "You're not telling me everything. I can tell." He paused. "Is it a woman?"

Blain raised his glass of Scotch and sipped at it.

"I'd rather not get into that," he said in a low voice. Bud wasn't surprised; he had been privy to most of the details of Blain's life in the past ten years, but Blain had remained steadfastly closemouthed about his romantic life. Bud had never really understood that; most men he knew took every opportunity to flaunt their sexual conquests, and Blain, he was positive, had had many to his credit. Yet, Blain had never let anyone get remotely close to that part of his life, Bud Stamfeld included.

"Well, all right," Bud conceded, crushing out his cigarette. "No problem with the rest of the season, is there?"

"Of course not. We've never had a better go at the championship. You think I'd give that up?" He hesitated, then said carefully, "But, look, I'd like to keep this out of the press until just before the last game, all right?"

"Deal," Bud agreed. He owed at least that much to Pearson after all the trouble-free years. He reached for the check as the waiter placed it on the table, but Blain snatched it up.

"It's on me," he said, reaching into his back pocket for his wallet.

Bud made no objections and he downed the rest of his Manhattan. Blain's retirement meant a great deal more than the loss of a client; he was losing one hell of a fine relationship.

Bobbi's breathing was ragged as she set the basket of clean clothes down beside the front door. She reached in to the back pocket of her jeans for the key, and as she let herself in the memory of the last wash day came back to her. She hadn't had to lift a thing, and the chore had been almost fun with Blain there helping.

This day had been the same old drag of a routine. Naturally she had taken the stairs instead of the poky elevator, and the effect was like running a fifty-yard dash, what with the pounds of laundry she had to cart back and forth. At least she had something to look forward to that night. Ralph had said he would pick her up at six thirty, so she still had time to snitch a well-deserved nap before then. She had awakened early that morning; an increasingly common and irritating occurrence of late. After having to get up at an absolutely ungodly hour all week long, it was disheartening to find herself awakening at the same time on one of her two precious days off.

After putting away the neatly folded and stacked

bundle of clothes, Bobbi stepped out of her jeans and T-shirt and closed the curtain at her bedroom window. She felt gloriously tired and her mind quickly submitted to the demands of her body.

Ralph had suggested the movie they were watching, and Bobbi sat through most of it simply staring at the screen, neither seeing nor absorbing any of the dialogue. What was the last movie she had watched? Oh, yes, she thought, smiling inwardly, the Woody Allen one... the one she and Blain had watched in—

She slammed the door shut on that thought, forcing herself to at least listen to enough of the movie to be able to carry on a decent conversation about it with Ralph later.

They ate at an Italian restaurant afterward, and the conversation did indeed cover the subject of the movie, in addition to a fair amount of shoptalk. Ralph's manner seemed a good deal more subdued than the last time they had gone out, but Bobbi assumed he was concerned about his mother's welfare.

He was truly quiet during the ride home, and Bobbi felt a few moments of distinct discomfort. As much as she had enjoyed his company, there was the distinct feeling of something missing, although she couldn't pin down either what it was or the cause of it. Of all the men she had ever dated, Ralph alone possessed all the ingredients she needed—*required*—in the man she would someday marry. And with her twenty-seventh birthday right around the corner—the following week, in fact—the knowledge took on even greater importance.

"Would you like to come in?" Bobbi asked Ralph as they stood on her landing.

Ralph adjusted his glasses and stood rather uncomfortably with his hands in his pockets. "I don't think so. I—"

Bobbi stared curiously at him. "Ralph, is something wrong?"

He glanced up at her with a startled expression.

"Is it about your mother?" Bobbi clarified. "Is she really all right?"

"Yes, yes...she's fine. Or will be in a few weeks." Ralph's expression and tone seemed relieved, and Bobbi was puzzled by the sudden change.

"You seem...I don't know, preoccupied about something."

Ralph shrugged and jiggled the coins in his pants pockets. His suit jacket was pulled back, revealing the vest he wore beneath. Actually, he really was an attractive man, Bobbi thought...in a dignified way.

"I guess I'm tired," he said finally. "I haven't been getting enough sleep this past week."

Bobbi smiled sympathetically. "You should have said something. We didn't have to go out tonight."

"Oh, no. I enjoyed it...really." He sounded earnest, but still there was something... She couldn't define it really, some peculiar glint in his eyes.

Suddenly his hands left his pockets and grasped Bobbi's upper arms through the sleeves of her dress and he pulled her to him. Hiding her surprise at the sudden move, Bobbi acquiesced, closing her eyes as his lips planted firmly against her own. Ralph knew very well the technique of kissing, there was no questioning that, but once again Bobbi experienced the sensation of something missing. The kiss was comfortable and nice... but that was all. When at last he pulled back, he peered down at her through the glasses he had forgotten to remove and smiled rather nervously.

"We'll have to do this again sometime," he said.

Bobbi smiled back at him and turned the knob to the apartment door. "I'd really like that, Ralph." She stepped inside the apartment and said, "Drive carefully and get a lot of sleep."

"I intend to," Ralph said. "See you Monday."

"Bye."

Bobbi shut the door and stood with her back to it for a long, thoughtful moment. She *had* had a nice time, she repeated to herself. A wholesome, nice time, with the right guy.

She drew in a deep breath and let it out slowly. The vague, inexplicable emptiness she felt inside would not be there forever. Time would take care of that.

And Ralph, of course.

The sound filtered through gradually to her conscious mind; she wasn't sure if it was part of her dream or not. Then suddenly her eyes flew open and her entire body went rigid as the sound became more distinct.

A click, a familiar creak, then the same click. By then Bobbi's heart was thumping wildly, yet still she couldn't move. Then she heard clearly the footsteps on the plush carpeting in the living room, and her arm shot out from under the covers to grab the telephone receiver. Her fingers punched jaggedly as she frantically tried to call Mary Beth. The line was busy. At this time of night!

Then suddenly she sat straight up, the familiar whistle adding a spark of anger to the riveting fear.

There was a light rap on her door, then "Bobbi?"

Bobbi reached up and ran her hands down the sides of her face. *I don't believe this,* she thought, slowly shaking her head.

"Bobbi? Are you awake?" The door opened, and Blain's head popped around it.

Bobbi reached over to switch on the light, then stared at him in stunned disbelief, completely surprised that she could find such a measure of calm, considering her galloping heart rate.

"No, I'm really asleep, and fortunately this is just a bad dream."

Blain smiled somewhat sheepishly and opened the door all the way. He remained inside the doorway, ducking his head as he leaned his lanky form against the doorframe.

"You don't look very asleep to me," he said with a grin.

At that Bobbi shot out of bed, heedless of the T-shirt she wore, which came to barely below her hips. Gone was any vestige of sleepiness, replaced by an overwhelming urge to strike out against the unbelievably cool man who had just managed to frighten her out of her wits.

"How in the hell did you get in here?" she demanded, glaring at him as his gaze traveled slowly upward from her bare legs to her seething features.

"Hmmm?"

"I said, how— Oh! Damn you." Blain was holding up the key he had purloined before he left the last time he stayed there. She'd forgotten all about it.

"Tsk, tsk. A lady in such...shall we say, incomplete attire is not in the position to make such heartfelt invectives."

"You got that right, buddy." Snatching up a robe, she threw it on in a huff and turned back to him. "About the heartfelt bit." Cocking her head to one side, she added, "And now that we've gotten the mode of operation for this break-in out of the way, perhaps you wouldn't mind revealing the reason, or reasons, as the case may be."

Lazily Blain crossed one ankle over the other, hooking his thumbs in the pockets of his corduroys. "We had a few days off, so I flew in to check on things at the town house."

Bobbi's eyes narrowed and she smiled sardonically. "Ah, yes, the lonely tenant. Geez, you just have 'em stashed everywhere, don't you?"

Blain appeared amused and frowned slightly as he said, "Not that I owe any explanations, but just to set the record straight, I'm not the type to fool around with another man's property...especially when the man happens to be a good friend."

Bobbi raised her head a bit and rolled her tongue along the inside of one cheek. "What is that supposed to mean?"

"Marielle is Hank Melcromb's girl friend. She's staying there until their wedding at the end of the summer."

"And who, may I ask, is he?"

"One of my teammates. I'd like for you to meet him sometime. You'd really like him. In fact, he was coming over with me tonight—"

"What! Blain Pearson, you wouldn't dare bring that man over here in the middle of the—"

Blain rolled his eyes and said, "Cool it, would ya? I said he *was* coming with me. But he couldn't make it."

Bobbi relaxed visibly. "Thank God." What a lifestyle they all led. Cavorting around in the middle of the night as if it were the most natural thing in the world. Well, it wasn't, not for her anyway.

"Listen, you may be able to flit around at all times of the day, but in case you didn't know it, I'm a working girl. I have to get up at five A.M., and it is now one thirty."

"That doesn't sound like the invitation I was anticipating." Blain glanced pointedly at Bobbi's mussed bed.

"Your anticipation happens to get you nowhere but the couch tonight, Mr. Pearson."

At the disappointed expression on his face Bobbi almost chuckled; he really did look crestfallen. All for the good as far as she was concerned. He needed to learn he couldn't just barge in on her like that and expect carte blanche treatment. Quickly she whisked past him and into the hallway. Opening the linen closet, she removed blankets and pillows, then walked into the living room and plopped them onto the couch.

Blain had followed and his eyes went from the heap on the couch to her determined face

"You wanted a place to stay," she said, raising her eyebrows haughtily as she walked past him, "you got it."

Blain's shoulders shrugged visibly and he looked at her with genuine regret. Apparently she meant business. Such a waste... such a beautiful waste.

Bobbi breezed past him and down the hallway to her bedroom, then hesitated with one hand on the doorknob. "Oh, by the way, do you want me to wake you up when I get up?"

"I'm sure you will anyway," Blain muttered.

"See you in the morning, then," she called back gaily and shut the door firmly behind her. The only other sound he heard out of her that night was the click of the lock.

The insides of Bobbi's eyelids were orange, and for a moment she wondered what was so strange about it. Then her eyes popped open and she stared in disbelief at the sunlight streaming through her window. Rolling onto her side, she grabbed the clock and stared in horrified amazement at the hour. Eight o'clock! Where was her head? Then she remembered. She had kept punching the doze switch until the damn thing gave up.

She sprung out of bed and dashed out into the hallway and into the bathroom. Hurriedly she switched on the hot water in the tub for her shower, then raced back out into the hallway. She could put on some water for a cup of coffee while—

She stopped dead in her tracks, her lips parting involuntarily as her eyes riveted on Blain's sleeping

figure on her couch. Good God! She'd forgotten all—
The lazy bum! He was responsible for this. This was
the second time he'd made her late for work. It was a
damn good thing she wasn't responsible for the car
pool that week.

Just then Blain turned onto his side and yawned. He
opened his eyes and smiled as he saw her standing
there.

"Hey, pip-squeak. Good morning."

Bobbi stomped over to the edge of the couch and
glared down at him. Despite her anger she couldn't
help but notice the picture he presented. The pillow-
case had creased one cheek, and his hair was in wild
disarray, pushed down onto his forehead. His eyelids
were half closed and his blue eyes peeping out took on
the sexiest appeal.

"Good morning, my foot. Damn it, Blain, it's eight
o'clock. I'm going to be an hour late for work."

"Hmmm. That's too bad," he said, then opened
his mouth wide to yawn long and hard.

"Stop that," Bobbi commanded, frustrated. "You
don't even care. This is the second time you've made
me late for work. In one month! That doesn't look too
hot on my record, you know."

Blain frowned and regarded her for a moment.
"Hmmm. I have an idea."

Bobbi was in the kitchen then, filling up the kettle
with water. "Like what?"

"Well, if you call in sick, then you'll miss the whole
day, and not just show up late. That way it might not
look so bad. On your record."

Bobbi said nothing for a moment. He was right

about that, but— "That's ridiculous. I have to go in today. I've got a lot to do."

Blain sat up and pulled the covers up over his lap. He was bare-chested, and she could only wonder what, if anything, he had on underneath the blanket. He shoved one hand through his hair and said, "Yeah, well, you've got a lot to do here also."

"What are you talking about?"

Blain hooked a thumb behind him. "First of all, your water is still running."

Bobbi sighed in vexation and raced out of the room. She returned to the kitchen and poured herself a glass of grapefruit juice.

"You still haven't bought a thing for that fancy kitchen of yours. I swear I've never seen such an empty place."

"I presume you're speaking of food."

"Precisely."

"Whatever that has to do with my missing work today I'll never guess."

"You need to get your buns to the grocery store, that's what it has to do with it."

Bobbi made a surly face and finished off the grapefruit juice. Glancing up at the wall clock, she suddenly felt like giving in. What would be the point of going in? She felt disoriented anyway . . . and she'd never get a thing done.

Blain took advantage of her momentary indecision and hastily interjected, "We can eat breakfast on the way, then do the shopping. I'll drop you off here afterward while I check on the town house. Then supper tonight at the restaurant of your choice."

Bobbi shook her head ruefully before a tiny smile crept across her lips. He had her there and he knew it. "All right, you bummer, you win. This time."

At that Blain smiled broadly and wiggled his eyebrows a la Groucho Marx, and Bobbi had to laugh.

They ate huge breakfasts at a pancake house, then lingered over coffee, reading the newspaper and taking turns reading each other particularly interesting or humorous stories.

The grocery store Blain chose was almost empty, and for once Bobbi found it a surprisingly enjoyable experience. Blain practically wiped out the shelves, and when there was absolutely no wait at the checkout counter, Bobbi was almost ecstatic. She snickered as she and Blain began unloading the basket full of items. Included were three boxes of Froot Loops and two of Cap'n Crunch.

"What happened to the health food kick?" Bobbi asked, cocking one eyebrow as she grinned at him.

Blain looked at her as though she had suddenly forgotten her own name. "For the munchies, of course."

Once again Bobbi found a highly dislikable chore quite enjoyable with Blain taking charge. By the time they got back to her apartment she was in the mood to really dig in and take care of other chores that usually stacked up and waited until the weekend for her attention.

Blain was back by five o'clock, and after dressing, they set out for Maryland, to the same country restaurant they'd dined at the first time. It was a lovely evening and by the end of it Bobbi had quite forgotten what she would have normally been doing that day. It was easy to be at ease with Blain, she rediscovered. He was so natural, so unpretentious, she couldn't think of being any other way with him.

Blain slept that night in far more comfort than the previous one. The couch went untouched as they slept peacefully in her bed, Bobbi curled up within the arc of his long frame, like two spoons nestled side by side. Their lovemaking was swift and greedy at first, pulsing with the heat of pent-up passion each was more than ready to dispel. Afterward, Bobbi rolled onto her stomach, and Blain's hands absently stroked the back of her neck. Bobbi groaned in blissful serenity, and his hands slipped downward to her shoulders; soon he was half sitting beside her, admiring the sweetly proportioned curves of her small form, allowing his hands to continue the massage, which was sheer delight for Bobbi.

He kneaded her shoulders, then, firmly pressing his thumbs along either side of her spine, drew a line up and down the center of her back, spreading his fingers wide to squeeze her rib cage. Then he was rubbing her firm, perfectly rounded buttocks, and the ever-glowing coal of desire within her ignited into a flickering, spreading flame. Moaning softly, Bobbi turned over, reaching out to Blain and pulling him down onto her. His body wasted no time in joining with hers, and together they savored, slowly that time, the sweet ecstasy of physical union.

It was a glorious experience, Blain's surprise visit, and Bobbi found herself wishing it could have happened more often. Yet, she knew, in her deepest soul, that it couldn't...and probably wouldn't. The next morning Blain was gone again. As quickly as he appeared into her life, he vanished out of it. Bobbi was left with an anxious feeling in the pit of her stomach, one she could hardly attempt to assuage. That was what Blain Pearson was all about; a mere temporary diversion in her life. The fact that she was probably becoming more emotionally involved than was prudent nagged constantly at the edges of her consciousness.

She knew it would be impossible to go on that way, indeed an absolutely ridiculous situation. She'd simply have to do something about it. Soon.

Chapter Thirteen

Bobbi managed to make it through the next week by working herself to a frazzle, involving herself to an almost unnecessary degree in the cases to which she was assigned. The coming Saturday was her birthday, and the thought of it made her more nervous by the hour.

It was ridiculous; she had never felt that uptight about a birthday in her entire life. For some reason, though, she couldn't manage to deal with the strange pressure, the sensation that her life had come up for review and that she needed to really get down to basics as far as how she wanted to live the rest of it.

Blain had hit the nail on the head in his assessment of her suffering from classical burn-out syndrome. She had been ambitious to the point of mania, and what good had it done? Somehow the work that had been fulfilling for the past year and a half was rapidly going stale. Only by immersing herself in it to an inordinate degree was she able to ignore her dissatisfaction.

But, she questioned herself, was it the job itself or

the dissatisfaction with her personal life that bothered her so? Twenty-seven was not old; common sense told her that no particular age was really old. It was how one reacted to one's age that counted. Admittedly she wasn't reacting so well. Not at all.

Blain's image came flooding back to her and she couldn't help the telltale lurch of her heart. Then Ralph's face floated into her mind, reminding her sharply of the differences between the two men. The former gave her no assurances whatsoever; indeed, the only assurance she had was of the inconsistency, the impracticality of their relationship. The latter, of course, was by far the more reasonable, the more sensible.

However, she could not continue to play both sides of the fence. Other women might find an egotistical pleasure in dating two men simultaneously, but she would not get involved in such a setup. Despite her undeniable physical attraction to Blain, the simple hard fact still remained: the two of them were completely wrong for one another. And with the news she'd gotten from the leasing agency that day, there was no longer an outside factor linking their lives. Blain's car would be returned within the next couple of days; all that remained was for her to notify him of the fact, and that would be the end of it. So, she decided, it would definitely be the wiser course to pursue the one relationship she knew to be strong enough to eventually lead to a lasting marriage.

Buoyed up by the positive thought, she reminisced over the events of the week so far. She and Ralph had shared lunch together every day as usual. She hadn't reminded him of her coming birthday, but she would bring it up the following day, and they could make plans to celebrate the occasion.

Blain raked a hand through his hair; he needed a cut soon. He'd have to see about getting one in the hotel's barber shop. Shirking off his clothes, he crossed the room and entered the bathroom, turning on the taps to let the hot water run before he stepped in for a shower.

His thoughts returned to the matter he was finding especially difficult to ignore that had been on his mind almost night and day of late; tiny, incorrigible, sensuous Bobbi Morrow. Who would have ever thought he'd end up falling in love with such a firecracker of a woman?

Yet he had. It was obvious she cared for him, perhaps not as deeply as he did for her, but he felt sure that was just a matter of time. In a funny sort of way they were made for one another, he knew it as well as he knew his own name.

All he needed was time with her, time to explain his plans for the future, time to simply be with her and let the relationship develop. But, just then, time was the one element he was most deficient in. In another three weeks he'd have his mind made up about which coaching position he'd accept, and the season would be over for him. The thought of retiring should have filled him with nostalgia, but considering the future that awaited him—a life with Bobbi—the past he was leaving behind paled by comparison.

The telephone was ringing as he stepped out of the

shower, and after briskly rubbing down his damp skin, he wrapped the large towel around his waist and secured it snugly. Grabbing another, he patted the back of his neck as he walked into the bedroom and picked up the telephone.

"Hello?"

"Blain, old man, how's it going?"

Blain frowned, then recognized the almost forgotten voice of his old college buddy.

"John?"

"Yeah, it's me! I read you were in town and tracked you down. Don't ask me how—it wasn't that easy. Anyway, I thought I'd give you a call and see what you've been up to lately. Besides what I read, of course."

Blain let the towel hang around his neck and he sat down on the edge of the bed. "Well, if this doesn't beat everything. I haven't heard from you in so long, I almost didn't recognize your voice."

"Just the same old me. Haven't changed much. Oh, well, a few pounds here and there, but still pretty much the same."

"Where are you living now?"

"In Long Beach. My wife and I have a couple of preschoolers now. Boy and a girl."

Blain could almost see the smug pride on John's ruddy face, and he had to grin. Gone were the days of bachelorhood, that was for sure.

"So, Don Juan has settled down," he teased. "Will wonders never cease."

John chuckled. "We can't all be wandering Romeos like yourself, you know."

Blain would have told him those days were soon to be gone from his own life, but he held his tongue. In time, he thought, in time.

"So how long will you be in L.A.?" John was asking.

"Through the weekend."

"Good. Then you can come out to the house and meet the family. Suzanne would love to meet you. The kids, too. How about Saturday night?"

Blain laughed. "Same old John. Don't waste any time getting straight to the point. But, yes, I'd love to see you and meet your brood. Just give me directions and the time, and we have a date."

"Hmmm. Well, there's a catch, you see."

"Uh-huh."

John let out a sigh. "Well, Suzanne's sister has been visiting with us for the past couple of weeks, and Suzanne thought if you were willing, we could drive in to L.A. and meet you. Have supper somewhere, then drive out to the house for a nightcap. You could even stay over if you like."

Blain scratched his jaw thoughtfully. He would have preferred meeting them there instead. "Okay," he agreed finally. "I'm staying at the Sheraton, southeast. I'll meet you in the lobby. What time?"

"Say around seven?"

"Sounds fine."

"Good. See you then."

"Good-bye."

Blain hung up the phone and stood with both hands clutching either end of the towel hanging around his neck. Not exactly the sort of evening he had hoped for, but it was better than doing nothing. And he really did look forward to seeing John.

Bobbi almost smacked right into Ralph as she rounded the corner of the corridor on the way to her office.

"Ralph! Sorry about that, but I wasn't looking where I was going."

Ralph smiled as he let his hand drop from its protective hold on Bobbi's upper arm. "You seem to be in a big hurry, too," he commented.

Bobbi shrugged and hugged the stack of folders she was carrying to her chest. "Not really." She grinned wryly. "As a matter of fact, the only thing I'm in a hurry about is lunch. I haven't had a thing to eat this morning and I'm starving."

Ralph checked his wristwatch. "It's almost eleven thirty. Why don't you leave a little early today and I'll take you out for some fantastic barbecue."

Bobbi's expression brightened considerably. "Now, that sounds like a fantastic idea."

"I'll meet you at your office in a few minutes."

"All right."

Whatever would she do without him? Bobbi wondered as she made her way back to her office. Ralph was the only person making her days at work bearable of late, and she was absolutely depending on him for the coming weekend. Mary Beth had announced excitedly that she and Rick would be visiting some friends of his in New York, and Bobbi had experienced a twinge of envy for the other woman's life at that point. She was always *doing* something, whereas Bobbi was constantly *waiting* for something to happen, almost having to create it herself. But not for long, she reassured herself. It was only a matter of time until she had things more firmly in hand. Once things were squared away as far as she and Ralph were concerned, her life would proceed the way it was supposed to.

Ralph was in an unusually amiable mood during lunch, but it was not until they were back at AMAC that he revealed he would be taking off early Friday to fly down to Florida to see his mother. Bobbi was taken off guard by the news, and for a moment she didn't know what to say. The disappointment stung, although she was not about to display her emotions then. Feeling terribly selfish, she expressed her good wishes for Ralph's mother and kept her expression carefully sympathetic.

By Friday night Bobbi was absolutely miserable. She honestly couldn't remember a time in her life when she had felt so emotionally bereft. When her mother called that evening from Richmond, it was all she could do to keep the lump in her throat from dissolving into an embarrassing sobbing spell. She informed her mother that she would be looking for the present her mother had sent that morning and she expressed her best wishes to her father also.

Dressed in her velour robe, she wandered aimlessly about the apartment, flipped through the television guide, and then the remote control, hoping something, anything, might grab her attention and give her at least a couple of hours' worth of respite from the attack of loneliness.

As she sunk down onto the couch and sipped at the glass of wine she had poured herself, her eyes wandered everywhere but the television screen. That night especially, it seemed, the sensation she had noticed ever since Blain had left the apartment assaulted her full force. She just couldn't shake the feeling that the apartment she had invested so much time and effort on, developing her own personal, comforting touch, was deficient of the warmth and homeyness he had instilled with his very presence.

It was as though he had implanted his unique aura within everything around her; the couch she was reclining on, the kitchen, the bathroom, the very robe she was wearing. She even ate breakfast every day because of him, and washing clothes alone was more of a bore than ever. Then memories of the weekend in Dallas came back, and of the night he'd surprised her—even angered her—all of which made her all the more sad.

Why, why couldn't she stop thinking of him! Slowly a minuscule tear trickled down her cheek, and she licked the salty drop from the corner of her mouth. Why did Ralph have to go out of town that weekend? And Mary Beth, too? Where were her friends when she needed them? she thought resentfully, feeling every bit the baby she was acting like.

Yet all of that had nothing to do with the fact that she still needed to get in touch with Blain. Just why she was putting it off she didn't care to analyze at that moment. He'd mentioned his schedule the last time he'd been there and had even told her where he normally stayed while in L.A. So why didn't she just pick up the damn phone and call?

The years seemed to peel away as Blain and John related one old story after another. Nothing much had changed about his old buddy, Blain discovered, except, of course, that he had settled down a great deal, much of it due to his wife, Suzanne, who, in Blain's opinion, was perfectly suited to him.

Suzanne's younger sister, Lori, was prettier than Suzanne and possessed a poise and sophistication that presented an attractive package. A tall brunette, she was gracefully slender, almost too slender. It was later revealed that her ambition was to model professionally. She was well on her way as far as self-discipline with food was concerned, that was certain. Throughout the course of the evening, which was filled with much enjoyable conversation and reminiscing, Blain nevertheless found his initial attraction for the young woman waning rapidly. Her obvious preoccupation with her looks was annoying; toying with the food on her plate, she looked as if she feared instant obesity if she consumed more than a few forkfuls.

Nevertheless he pretended to be taken with her, relying on the old instincts and tactics that had always worked so well in the past. A certain image flickered before his mind's eye; that of a cinnamon-haired pixie, and he felt a certain clutching in his gut. Dammit! why did they have to be so far apart? Suddenly he knew he couldn't bear another night alone in that fancy-ass hotel room. If he couldn't have her...

"Lori's staying at the Sheraton too, Blain," Suzanne was saying.

"Oh? I thought you were visiting...."

"Yes, I have been," Lori said, smiling brightly.

"But I have business appointments for the next couple of days in L.A., then I'm flying out to San Francisco."

"Then why don't I give you a lift tonight?" Blain offered, smiling guilelessly.

Lori agreed, and Blain lifted his glass to his lips, the knowing looks exchanged between John and Suzanne not escaping his attention. Well, so what? he thought dryly, all too aware of the foul temper that suddenly worsened within him.

Bobbi kicked the covers restlessly down to the bottom of the bed, her consciousness somewhere between a state of half sleep and an irritated wakefulness. She'd made it through the ridiculously long day in the same depressed state that had taken over the day before. More than anything in the world Bobbi hated being depressed. Normally she would have fought it tooth and nail, applying all her powers of positive thinking to get her out of the miserable state of mind.

Yet she had simply given in to it that day. Celebrating a birthday alone was bad enough under any circumstances, but this one held a certain significance that made the situation even more untenable. She had finally reached the formidable old age of twenty-seven. Oddly enough the sky did not fall, and her appearance in the mirror did not reveal any new or telling signs of aging. Was she becoming neurotic, or was everyone affected with a certain birthday as this one was affecting her? Still, the inescapable fact was that the climb had begun. In three short years—which would seem, no doubt, more like a few months—she would be thirty. And what did she have to show for it? Earlier she would have claimed the relative success she had achieved in her job, but that had long since been on a losing streak as far as she was concerned.

The fact that she had nothing in her personal life to be proud of or even satisfied with nagged at her like a sore, infected tooth. She simply had to do something about it, that was all there was to it! And she would, she reminded herself. She and Ralph were already on the road to a closer, more committed relationship. That was enough for now, she averred to herself.

Her mind, however, would simply not stop churning. Regardless of her positive thinking concerning Ralph, there was still that one matter with Blain to clear up. Suddenly she sat up and shoved her hands through her hair. She gave a cursory glance at the lighted alarm clock, then switched on the bedside lamp. What the hell, she might as well get it over with and call him up to let him know about the Corvette. Damn that stupid Corvette! Her life had been fine until *it* had appeared!

She scooted up in the bed as information located the number to the Sheraton, then reached over to jot it down quickly. It was 11 P.M. there she noted, glancing at the alarm clock as she listened to the scratchy connection. Nervously she twisted the cord around her hand as she waited for the call to transfer through to Blain's room.

A click sounded as the receiver was picked up on the other end, and Bobbi was aware of a familiar lurch in her stomach. Incredible how the man did these things to her.

"Hello?" The voice was a woman's, soft and low as a cat's purr.

Bobbi swallowed and felt the lurch become a shaft of sickening dread. She didn't want to know this... although she'd really known it all along, hadn't she?

"Y-yes, I'm trying to reach Mr. Blain Pearson." Perhaps... perhaps she'd gotten the wrong room.

"Oh. All right. Just a minute." The purr was edged with annoyance, and Bobbi's eyes narrowed resentfully. So she *had* gotten the right connection. And who the hell was *she*? But then, what difference did it make? One of many.

"No," she almost barked the word. "That's all right. Just give him a message."

"Yes?" More annoyance.

"Tell him that his car is back now. He can pick it up anytime."

"That's it?"

"Yes."

She hung up, the thick, nauseating dread having quickly solidified into a cold lump of hard reality. No more wondering or suspicions. She *knew.* Knew then more than ever how very, very little the two of them had in common, how ridiculous a waste of time their little fling had been.

He may have the capacity to be casual about their relationship, easily moving in and out of other ones the same way he moved in and out of her life, but she didn't. She never would.

Slowly she lay back down, her gaze riveting on the ceiling unseeingly. So it was over. Done. Finished, as far as she was concerned. Oh, no doubt in his mind things would continue as they had before, and even as she thought it the telephone rang...and rang...and rang.

And Bobbi just ignored it as she turned onto her side, one fat tear dripping slowly down her cheek and onto the bed. The ringing stopped then and started again. She knew it was Blain and she refused to answer. Just as she would refuse to ever speak to him again. What was the point in it? They were finished.

Gradually a deep, sickening depression overtook her; a remorseful anger directed at herself for ever having let him into her life in the first place.

Chapter Fourteen

Bobbi watched as the sales clerk covered the lavender crepe de chine dress with a protective plastic bag, the store's prestigious logo printed boldly across both sides. The amount she had just paid for the garment exceeded anything she'd ever spent on something to be worn on but a few choice occasions, but then that *was* what she was buying it for.

"Thank you," she said, smiling as the saleswoman handed her the dress. Turning, her eyes swept the elegantly decorated couture salon of the expensive department store, stopping as she spotted Mary Beth next door in the fur gallery, gazing longingly as a severely made-up, bleached-blond woman was casually trying on several mink coats.

Bobbi walked up behind her friend and, employing a fastuous tone, said, "Can I help you find something, madam?"

Mary Beth turned, startled to see it was only Bobbi standing there. "No, thank you," she replied in an equally haughty tone, "I don't see anything I really care for.'' Tilting her head upward, she sniffed, pursing her lips together.

Bobbi chuckled lightly, then said, "Come on, let's get out of here. The atmosphere's so stuffy, I can hardly breathe."

Their footsteps, muffled initially by the thick iceblue carpeting, clicked smartly as they walked along the marble floor toward the escalators.

Mary Beth glanced at the bag Bobbi was carrying and shook her head. "I can't believe you just spent all that money. I would have *died* if I had to write a check for that amount."

Bobbi drew in a shuddery breath. "It does kind of feel weird. But it's done, and I'm glad I did it. I don't care about the money; it makes me feel good to splurge like this."

Mary Beth shrugged. "Well, where to now?"

"Shoes. First floor."

"You're not gonna get away with this, you know," Mary Beth warned as they walked toward the shoe department. "You dragged me all the way over here, and not for nothing. I want to know what's got you so fired up that—"

"All right, all right," Bobbi conceded. Turning, she handed the garment bag to her friend. "Here, hold this for me, will you, while I'm trying on shoes? And okay, we'll talk about it over over lunch."

Mary Beth hung the bag over her arm and sauntered off, apparently appeased by Bobbi's answer. Fortunately Bobbi's shoe size was in stock, and with the box tucked securely under her arm, she found Mary Beth, who was now browsing in the cosmetic department.

The restaurant they'd decided on had just opened its doors for lunch, so Bobbi and Mary Beth were seated immediately. Both women ordered glasses of white wine, and as they sipped and ate the salads that preceded their entrées, Mary Beth immediately launched into the subject she'd been waiting to discuss.

"Now, just what is this all about, Bobbi? For the last couple of weeks you've been a regular drag if there ever was one. Now all of a sudden you go out and spend a downright *fortune* on a dress you'll hardly ever wear, with shoes to match." Accepting the piece of French bread Bobbi had sliced, Mary Beth buttered it, her eyes studying Bobbi's thoughtfully. She took a bite, chewed appreciatively, then swallowed. Wiping a crumb from one corner of her mouth, she asked, "Well?"

Bobbi finished her own mouthful of salad and sipped her wine. She looked up at her friend with a simple forthright expression. "I'm entertaining tonight."

"Entertaining who?"

"Whom," Bobbi corrected.

"Whatever," Mary Beth shrugged and frowned. "Come on, Bobbi, stop playing games." Suddenly her eyes widened and she blurted out, "Don't tell me! You're seeing *him*! I got the impression that was over." There was no mistaking the excitedness in Mary Beth's brown eyes.

Bobbi scowled. "What are you talking about?"

"Blain Pearson. He's back, and you're having him over for supper tonight. No wonder you went out and bought all that—"

"I'm *not* talking about him," Bobbi interrupted

brusquely, attributing the warm flush spreading up her neck and face to the effects of the wine.

Mary Beth looked distinctly disappointed. "Then, who—"

"I'm having a celebration supper for Ralph Goodman. He just got the news yesterday that he's been promoted to controller of his division."

Mary Beth's animated features drooped drastically.

"For *that* you're going to all this trouble?"

"Of course," Bobbi retorted defensively. "Ralph has worked long and hard for this position. He deserves it more than anyone, and besides..."

Mary Beth was attacking her salad now with renewed interest; what she had assumed was going to be an exciting, romantic discussion had just turned incredibly boring.

"And besides," Bobbi repeated, "there's more to his coming over than that."

"Oh? What?" Mary Beth glanced up, her attention mildly diverted from her preoccupation with the almost-finished salad.

Bobbi slanted her green gaze out the glass partition that looked onto the main corridor of the shopping mall. She hesitated for several seconds, and Mary Beth studied her features carefully.

"Well, he didn't say so directly, but Ralph did mention he had something important he wanted to discuss with me."

"I don't get it," Mary Beth stated bluntly.

Bobbi's gaze swung back to confront her friend's. "I'm fairly certain he's going to ask me to marry him."

Mary Beth's eyes widened and her jaw slackened in dismay.

"You're kidding," she stated flatly.

"No, I'm not kidding," Bobbi answered defensively.

"Ralph Goodman is going to ask you to marry him?"

"You sound as if it's a crime or something." Bobbi frowned.

"No, not a crime. Just the most ridiculous thing I've ever heard in my entire life."

Bobbi bristled, stunned by Mary Beth's blunt comment. She hadn't exactly expected all-out enthusiasm, but neither had she imagined Mary Beth would react quite so negatively. Forthrightness was one thing, but rudeness was another.

"That was uncalled-for," Bobbi said tersely.

Mary Beth's expression softened somewhat. "I didn't mean to upset you, Bobbi, but I'd be lying if I said I didn't mean it."

Bobbi's eyes narrowed. "Even knowing what you do about the way I feel for him?"

"Who?"

"Ralph, of course," Bobbi answered irritatedly.

"Oh." The waiter appeared and removed their empty salad plates, and Mary Beth nodded her head as he said their entrées would be out soon. Looking up at Bobbi, she said, "Actually, I *don't* know how you feel about him. You've never said that much about him, and I'm sorry, but I'm really shocked at what you've just told me. How can you say you're going to marry a man you've barely even dated?"

"But that's not true! We've gone out many times, but that isn't important. I've known Ralph since I've worked for AMAC—almost two years. We've been friends for a long time. I know what kind of man he is, what he's going to make of his life."

Mary Beth stared back at her friend with an expectant look. "Go on."

Bobbi gestured with one hand, palm upward. "What do you mean 'go on'? What more do I have to say?"

"I can think of plenty. That you love him, for one."

Bobbi swallowed and glanced away. "Of course I love him," she said, hearing the hollowness of her voice.

"You do?" Mary Beth asked doubtfully. "Since when?"

Bobbi's eyes swung back, and Mary Beth recognized the angry sparks flashing within the green depths.

"It doesn't matter since when. If I say I love him, that's all that matters. And besides, successful marriages have been built on far less."

The last comment convinced Mary Beth of what she had felt fairly sure about anyway. Bobbi Morrow was no more in love with Ralph Goodman than she was with the man in the moon. She hated to see what was happening to her friend; she was fooling no one but herself, and she wondered how long even that would last.

"Has he said anything about it yet? About getting married?"

Bobbi shook her head. "No. But that wouldn't be

like Ralph. If something is that important to him, it deserves more than just casual discussion."

"Well, he hasn't asked you yet, so you have time to really think it over."

"I *have* thought it over," Bobbi said emphatically. The waiter appeared just then with the rest of their order, but even the delicious, perfectly prepared seafood crepes did nothing to stimulate her already lagging appetite. Mary Beth, she noticed, had no such hesitation over her own meal and set about downing it hungrily.

"And I've made my decision," Bobbi continued firmly. "I am going to marry Ralph Goodman."

Mary Beth looked at her friend with a carefully blank expression. She'd never have predicted something this off-the-wall; Bobbi had always been the epitome of levelheadedness, never one to jump to conclusions or make hasty, reactionary decisions. There was obviously a good deal more to it than Bobbi was revealing, but the case was closed for now at least. Mary Beth mulled the matter over as they continued to eat in silence, then the idea came to her. Surely Blain Pearson had something to do with it! In spite of Bobbi's claims to the contrary, Mary Beth was still as certain as ever of her initial intuitiveness about the two of them having fallen in love. Was this what it was all about? Had something happened between them to cause Bobbi to want to marry someone else on the rebound? Love could do that to people; make the most practical person in the world do the most ridiculously stupid thing.

Which was exactly what, in Mary Beth's opinion,

Bobbi was about to do by agreeing to marry Ralph. She wished she could talk some sense into her friend's head, but there was little she could do about it right then. Ah, well, Mary Beth mused, hopefully she'd come to her senses in time. Pray God, she would.

Staring at her reflection in the full-length mirror of her closet door, Bobbi frowned slightly, turning this way and that to ascertain just exactly what it was she was displeased with. The lavender dress looked different somehow than when she'd tried it on that morning. More daring, she admitted wryly. The bodice was more revealing than she'd remembered, the demure ruffled neckline overshadowed by the way the material molded her breasts.

This wasn't the dress she should have chosen, it dawned on her suddenly. It most definitely wasn't the sort of thing Ralph would appreciate. Maybe Blain, but certainly not—

"To hell with him," Bobbi muttered aloud. "Who cares what sort of dress *he'd* like anyway." She stalked out of the room and into the bathroom to touch up the makeup she had already applied. It was Mary Beth's fault that she was even thinking of him; she'd done so well the last couple of weeks, wiping him out of her mind. What had begun as a pleasant day had taken a nose dive rapidly as soon as she and Mary Beth had had that ridiculous conversation at lunch. She'd been irritable the rest of the day, and it was all she could do to set her mind on getting ready. Determinedly she had set about marinating the steaks she'd paid a small fortune for, baking the carrot cake with her mother's special recipe, and taking care of a myriad other details for the elegant supper she'd planned.

Giving a final fluff to her hair, which she had curled and brushed out to a bouncy fullness, Bobbi made up her mind that enough was enough. She was simply going to have to get her emotions in hand. It wouldn't do at all to be in anything other than a pleasant mood when Ralph arrived. After all, it was a special occasion, and *she* had been the one to suggest that they celebrate over dinner at her apartment.

Ralph had flown back to Florida again for a couple of days last weekend, and Bobbi had to admire his devotion to his ailing, but recovering mother. She had picked him up at the airport Sunday night and they'd gone to supper. Ralph had never seemed more vivacious and full of himself, Bobbi had noticed as he carried on the bulk of the conversation, much of it having to do with how his parents were doing and how enjoyable the weather was at that time of year in Florida. She had taken him home to his town house that night, but it was late when they got there, so neither of them thought of extending the evening any further. They had stood at the rear of her car after Bobbi had retrieved his luggage, and as he searched his briefcase for the keys to his town house, he smiled warmly at her. Gently he'd placed his lips on her cheek for a moment, a tender, affectionate peck. Bobbi had thought then that surely she would never encounter another man so entirely respectful, so patient for the physical side of their relationship to develop.

Wrapping an apron around her waist then, she set about the last-minute preparations, but something about the material triggered her memory. Wasn't it the same one Blain had worn?... Scowling, she pushed the thought aside, focusing her attention on what she was doing.

Promptly at seven thirty the doorbell chimed, and Bobbi called out, "Just a minute." Hastily she popped the foil-covered French loaf into the oven and set the timer, then removed the apron and put it on the counter top.

Ralph had dressed casually and looked handsome in a preppy sense, in a pair of tan slacks and a dark brown crew-necked sweater over an eggshell-colored shirt. His dark brown hair had been recently cut and layered, a refreshing contrast to the usual squarish, one-length style he sported. All of his time in Florida had evidently not been spent inside at his mother's bedside. His pale skin had acquired a healthily bronzed tone. Bobbi couldn't remember a time she'd ever seen Ralph look so handsome and fit.

"Come in," Bobbi greeted him with a smile.

"Mmmm." Ralph sniffed the air appreciatively. "What's cookin'? Smells delicious."

"All sorts of goodies," Bobbi said, closing the door behind him as he walked into the living room.

"I like your place," Ralph said, his hands shoved into the pockets of his slacks, his head turning slowly as he looked around. "You're quite a decorator."

Bobbi laughed lightly. "Me? Hardly. I just pick up ideas from magazines, spend a lot of time browsing, then settle for something I can afford." Had he really never been here before? The question nipped at the back of her mind. How odd...

"Well, you've managed quite admirably in my opinion," Ralph said, sitting down on the edge of the couch.

"Thank you. Would you care for some wine?"

"Sure."

"Help yourself to the cheese and crackers. I'll be right back."

Uncorking a bottle of chilled Gewurztraminer, Bobbi noticed with chagrin that her hands were shaking slightly. How silly, she thought, withdrawing the cork and setting the bottle aside as she reached for a couple of wineglasses. But the shaking extended to her insides, which were quivering strangely. She filled the wineglasses and shifted her gaze to see that Ralph had settled back onto the couch and was leafing through a magazine. Discreetly she gulped down half a glassful, then filled it back up. That was totally uncharacteristic of her, she realized, but since she couldn't explain the sudden attack of nervousness, she might as well do something about it.

A warm tingling began in her empty stomach, the alcohol taking effect as she returned to the living room and set the glasses of wine down on the coffee table.

"Here you are," she said, sitting down on the love seat next to the couch. Sighing briefly, she said, "Well...how did your day go? As good as yesterday?"

Ralph laughed jovially. "Nothing could top yesterday. Unless, of course, I was offered a vice-presidency."

"You just might, you know," Bobbi flattered him, thinking how nice it was that he was a man of ambition; not an overpowering kind of ambition, but one that would certainly produce a good financial future.

They spoke then about the company and about matters relating to Ralph's promotion. Bobbi was attentive and carried her fair share of the conversation, but another part of her brain was working on an altogether different level. The true cause for the nervousness she was experiencing had to do with the other matter Ralph had alluded to when she had invited him over.

His manner, in spite of his relaxed outward appearance, was somewhat formal, considering all the time they had spent in one another's company. But then, Bobbi reflected, he must be twice as nervous as she was. There was absolutely no doubt in her mind what was on his; understandably he would wait until after supper to make the proposal she'd always known he would eventually get around to. That was all right, but she wished he would get it over with so they might relax and enjoy the meal.

The food and a second bottle of wine took care of the initial tenseness quite well, however. By the end of the main course, they both were almost completely relaxed with one another, laughing and talking while eating the carrot cake, which had turned out to be absolutely scrumptious.

The ring of the doorbell as they sat talking was an

almost foreign sound, and at first Bobbi didn't even hear it, Ralph having to point it out.

She frowned. "Now, who could that be?" she wondered aloud, thinking that it definitely wasn't Mary Beth; perhaps it was one of her neighbors. "Excuse me," she said as she got up and crossed the living room to the front door.

A bolt of lightning could not have struck more forcefully than the jolt she received as she opened the door.

Blain Pearson, all six feet five inches of him, stood on her doorstep, breathtakingly sexy in a pair of faded jeans that molded against his hips and hard thighs, his V-neck navy velour pullover revealing a matting of dark crisply curling chest hair. His ocean-blue eyes surveyed her from head to foot, taking in the elegant, incredibly sensuous dress she was wearing. He felt as if the inside of his gut was being pummeled as his mind conjured up a memory of what lay beneath the revealing lavender dress. He smiled broadly and withdrew the one hand that had remained behind his back, bringing it forward to present her with a bouquet of fresh daisies.

"I hope you like daisies, 'cause that's all I could find. They were out of roses."

Bobbi swallowed hard and stared for a moment at the flowers, her lovely wide eyes blinking erratically as she chewed on her lower lip. "Wha-what are you doing here?" she asked, almost choking over the words. Blain's sudden appearance was affecting her for more reasons than the fact that another man was in her apartment at that very moment. The physical reaction to his presence rose up to almost smothering proportions within her, visions of the nights they'd spent together darting through her mind in a most disconcerting fashion.

Blain cocked an eyebrow. "Aren't you going to ask me in?"

Bobbi hesitated, then stepped out onto the landing, pulling the door almost shut. "I'm surprised you didn't just barge in, like the last time." Crossing her arms over her chest, she added, "Well, did you get it?"

Blain's expression darkened with the move she'd just made; what was she in such a hurry to close the door for?

"Get what?"

"The car," Bobbi answered impatiently. Why did he have to do this to her? She'd gotten her message across repeatedly. Every time he'd called she'd simply slammed the phone down in his ear, not minding one bit if his eardrum shattered in the process.

"Yes. I picked it up yesterday." Blain frowned lightly. He'd expected anger, of course, but if she'd only invite him in, give him a chance to explain....

"So, then, what else are you here for? A game?"

Blain nodded. "Next Saturday." He paused, then said carefully, "We play in Boston...our last game. But that's not what I came here to talk to you about."

Bobbi looked at him. "Oh?"

Damn her cold bitchiness, Blain thought hotly, finding it difficult to put a leash on his emotional response to the encounter. But he wasn't about to give up at this point; not after all he'd been through to get here.

"It would be easier if we could go inside to talk," he suggested wryly. He gestured to his casual attire as he indicated her revealing, yet formal dress. "You'll have to excuse the way I'm dressed, but I—"

Bobbi interrupted, "I'm sorry, but we have nothing to talk about, and—you can't come in, Blain," she said. A surge of bittersweet emotion welled up within her as she said the words; she wanted him to leave, desperately, yet at the same time a pang of regret knifed through her, the pain so real, she could feel it.

"Why not?" he asked, his features matching the hardness in his tone.

Bobbi's gaze flickered for an instant, then focused squarely on his. "I have a guest."

Blain's action then shocked her totally. Taking one long-strided step, he raised one leg, and with his booted foot kicked open the door to the apartment, causing it to flail backward on its hinges and bounce back off the rubber doorstop. Ralph, who was partially hidden by the furniture, turned toward them, but the door had swung back to an almost closed position. However, it had opened long enough and wide enough for Blain to get a clear picture of what was taking place inside.

His imagination, which had been working overtime the past few weeks, could not have conjured up a more intimate picture than he observed in those few short seconds. Soft music, mellow candlelight, crumpled napkins atop the table, two empty bottles of wine . . . lovers enjoying a romantic evening alone.

The face that confronted Bobbi was alarmingly violent; dark, thunderous emotions contorted the handsome features, narrowing the sensuous mouth she'd known so intimately, flaring the nostrils of the straight nose in a way she had never seen before. His eyes deepened to a midnight blue as he lowered his gaze to the bunch of flowers he still held, as if unaware of how they came to be there.

"Blain, I—" Bobbi began haltingly, not having the slightest idea of what she meant to say.

"Sorry to interrupt your little rendezvous," Blain stated tonelessly, then smiled sarcastically. "But it wasn't necessary to make me feel like an ass."

"Make *you* feel like—"

"Forget it," he interrupted harshly, and his next movement startled Bobbi so that she jumped back a step, one hand grasping involuntarily at her throat. He flung the bouquet of daisies against the railing, the delicate white petals scattering about everywhere, then turned and muttered, "It doesn't make one hell of a difference anyway." His boots stomped noisily on the concrete landing, then clunked down the stairway two steps at a time.

Bobbi felt as if her entire body had been hooked up to some sort of vibrating machine, it was shaking so badly. A wild mixture of emotions swirled through her, and it was only with supreme effort that she managed to get a hold of herself, remembering that Ralph was waiting for her inside.

She must forget it immediately! It never happened! She had to ignore the bittersweet pain that still tore at her, erase the image of Blain's stunned, truly hurt expression when he'd discovered Ralph inside her apartment. It was for the best, she told herself resolutely. If it took something like that to convince him that there was absolutely nothing else to their relationship—except a past—then so be it.

Slowly Bobbi turned and placed her hand on the doorknob to push it open. The image of Blain's contorted face appeared unbidden in her mind's eye just then; never, never in a million years would she have believed that he would have reacted that way.

Ralph turned around and looked up at Bobbi as she entered the apartment. With a great deal of willpower and determination she had managed to restore an expression of composure to her features.

"Is everything all right?" Ralph asked in a concerned tone. "I didn't know what to think when the door flew open like that."

Bobbi waved a hand in the air and produced a chuckle. "I leaned against it accidentally. It was just a neighbor," she lied casually, resuming her seat across the table from Ralph. "He wanted to let me know he'd be going out of town tomorrow. I usually keep an eye on his apartment when he's away."

Ralph nodded, picked up his glass of wine, and drained it. He shifted as though uncomfortable, and after studying him a moment, Bobbi could see that indeed he was.

"Why don't we move to the living room?" she suggested, opening a third bottle of wine and refilling his glass and her own. She carried them, along with the bottle, into the living room.

Ralph followed and sat down on the couch, Bobbi preferring, for the moment, the love seat. Uncharacteristically Ralph cleared his throat, and it was obvious, even in the muted lighting, that his face had darkened to a rosy bronze. Bobbi looked at him curiously, his nervousness not doing a thing for her own, which was increasing by the moment.

"Bobbi, I—" Ralph began, then lifted his glass and drained it. Immediately Bobbi lifted the wine bottle to fill it once more, but Ralph held up a hand.

"No...no more. I've had more than enough." He smiled stiffly. "It was good, really."

"Thank you," Bobbi replied, forcing a smile.

Once more Ralph cleared his throat, then plunged right in with the next breath. "Bobbi, you remember I told you there was something very important I wanted to talk to you about tonight?"

Bobbi nodded once, sensing the strain he was under, wishing he'd get it over with and done with. "Yes," she prompted.

Ralph sat forward on the edge of the couch, rubbing the palms of his hands together as he spoke.

"Well..." He drew in a deep breath and looked up at her, his mouth widening into a grin that was reflected in his brown eyes. "I wanted you to be the first to know...I'm getting married next month."

Bobbi blinked once, then stared stupidly at him, her face muscles frozen as she took in the confusing words. "What?"

Ralph looked at her sheepishly. "I know what you must be thinking...why didn't I tell you about it before. But I couldn't—not until I was sure about everything."

Carefully masking her total shock, Bobbi asked in a small voice, "Sure about what?"

"About Rebecca. My fiancée." The palm rubbing

resumed for a moment, then stopped as Ralph continued, apparently a great deal more relaxed since he'd made the statement. "She wasn't sure when would be the best time to quit her job, and we just worked out the details this past Thursday. She'll be moving up here in about three weeks, and we'll be getting married a couple of weeks later."

Ralph pressed his lips together and looked expectantly at Bobbi; it was apparent that he was waiting for her comment, her congratulations. Bobbi remembered learning in an abnormal psychology class in college about the human mind being equipped with temporary methods of coping with traumatic or shocking situations. She'd had her share of both today, and her brain revealed its protective capability by allowing her normal self to stand back for the time being, delivering to center stage a personality Bobbi neither knew of nor particularly cared for, but which served the moment perfectly.

The "other" personality produced a heartwarming smile on her lips, which felt as frozen as ice, and she heard herself replying, "That's absolutely *fantastic,* Ralph. I couldn't be happier for you." She lifted her shoulders. "But when did all this happen?"

Ralph shook his head. "Actually, it all began a long time ago. Rebecca and I dated in college. We broke up right after graduation. I know I've never told you about it, I thought it best to forget the past completely. But, anyway, the first time I'd seen her in seven years was when I flew down to Florida to be with my mother for her operation."

"And the magic flame was rekindled with one heart-stopping look," Bobbi quipped.

Ralph chuckled. "Not quite. But suffice it to say we got back together again almost immediately. I didn't say anything about it before, because things weren't settled. But we managed to work things out the last couple of times I flew down."

"Not gonna waste any time, are you?" Bobbi teased.

"There's not really any reason to at this point."

Ralph had settled back on the couch by then, apparently totally at ease and warmed to his subject. By the end of the evening Bobbi had discovered a great deal more than she ever cared to about his wife-to-be, Rebecca.

Her legs were rubbery as she stood to walk with him to the door. She'd polished off the rest of the wine with no help from Ralph at all; a feat she would pay dearly for in the morning, there was no doubt about that. But just then she didn't care. It served her purpose quite well; she would have no problem getting to sleep, that was certain.

Ralph hesitated at the door, and Bobbi was sure her eyelids were going to shut permanently if he didn't leave soon.

"Bobbi, about—" Ralph shifted his weight and addressed her shoulder. "About our date—"

"What date?" Bobbi brought a hand up to her lips, successfully stifling a burp. Her vision was swimming, and Ralph looked really funny—like a brown cuddly teddy bear.

"The time we went to the movies and supper."

"Oh. *That* date," she said thickly, wondering whether the slur in her voice was as obvious as it sounded to her own ears.

"About—" Ralph chewed on his lower lip, and Bobbi wondered why in the world he was taking so long to take his leave. "About our kiss."

Bobbi stared back at him, trying to control the swaying her body had started; any moment she would be asleep on her feet. She was thoroughly soused!

Ralph cleared his throat. "I wasn't sure then about what was going to happen with Rebecca and myself. There was a time— Well, I'd always assumed that someday you and I—"

Bobbi leaned forward and whispered, "Shhh," placing two fingers over his mouth. "You don't have to say anything more. I know where you're comin' from, as they say."

Ralph's eyes brightened with relief at her words and he turned the doorknob, stopping, before he pulled the door ajar, to place his hands on Bobbi's shoulders and plant a smack on her cheek. "You're the greatest friend a guy could ever want, Bobbi."

Bobbi reached up unsteadily and tweaked his chin. "Same here."

"Well, good night," Ralph said as he opened the door. "And thanks for the supper. It was great." He stopped, bending down to pick something up. Bobbi's mouth contorted in a suppressed yawn, then froze as he turned and handed her the bouquet of wilted, badly damaged daisies.

"Wonder how those got here?" he said as he stepped onto the landing.

Bobbi managed a disinterested shrug. "Who knows? Well, good night, Ralph. See you Monday."

Ralph lifted a hand, then walked away. Bobbi shut the door slowly, the drooping flowers in her hand becoming a blur of yellow and white as she stared at them through a haze of tears. She swallowed hard, but the burning constriction in her throat remained as she dropped the bouquet onto the coffee table and stumbled to the bedroom, not bothering to remove the dress she had paid so dearly for.

Her eyelids closed within seconds, and the pain and the humiliation receded for a few merciful hours.

Chapter Fifteen

Awakening the next morning was the most physically painful thing Bobbi could ever remember experiencing. There had been times in her life before when she had drunk too much, but the agony she was feeling in gradually discovered bits and pieces was excruciating. The inside of her mouth felt like it was insulated with asbestos, she felt downright nauseated, but most of all her head pounded as though someone had dropped a ten-pound bowling ball on it. Whichever way she moved, one symptom or the other was exacerbated.

Groaning aloud, she turned onto her side, trying to remember just how much of the wine she had actually drunk. But the mere thought of it made her want to gag, so she put it out of her mind, only to be replaced by other equally nauseating thoughts.

Had all of yesterday really happened? Had her life really come to a screeching halt the way it seemed to have? God, it was too much to consider, and besides, it made her want to cry, which only made her head hurt more. Closing her eyes, she tried to lose herself to sleep once more, but it wouldn't come. A strange, vibrating sensation had crept over her nervous system and, after seriously considering it, she decided the only thing that might help even the slightest was to get up and take a hot shower.

Moving around made the agony worse at first, she discovered, but the stinging rays of the shower were mercifully restorative as she stood with her arms wrapped beneath her breasts, her back turned to the pelting massage of the water. It was a good thing that it was Sunday; she'd never have made it through a Monday morning like this.

Despite her temporarily successful attempt to push aside the thoughts weighing so heavily upon her mind, they filtered back in drips and drabs as she stood beneath the shower, oblivious to the inordinate amount of water she was using. There was no denying it, she had been a first-class fool in assuming all she had about Ralph's feelings toward her. *Best friend* was how he had termed it; how many times had she thought the same thing about him? One receives only as much as one gives, she thought wryly.

Turning, she faced the spray of steaming water as if to wash away all the regret, the foolishness. Closing her eyes, the sting of it felt good on her face and scalp, and she began to collect her thoughts in a more rational light. In all sincerity she was really happy for Ralph. He would make his Rebecca a fine husband, and she wished the best for both of them.

The hard-core fact of the matter was that she had been lying to Mary Beth—but most of all to herself—about being in love with Ralph. Deep within she must have sensed all along that nothing more than friendship would ever develop between the two of them. What didn't make sense at all was how she could have believed that she could *make* herself fall in love with him! A completely ludicrous notion. Realizing the extent of her stupidity, she recognized a distinct feeling of relief that Ralph had *not* asked her to marry him. It hadn't been what she'd wanted at all.

Her composure faltered, however, with the memory of what had occurred on the landing the night before. Blain's appearance had affected her infinitely more than anything that had ever happened between herself and Ralph. The attraction she felt for Blain had never dissipated; not one bit. Even now, despite everything, she wanted him so badly, it made her body ache from her head to her toes.

Like the fascination of discovery one senses upon watching the magical unfolding of a new morn, Bobbi became aware of a deeper meaning just then, a basic realization that contrasted drastically with her previous concept of her life. Simply stated, her pragmatic way of viewing most things did not always hold true. One did not simply order the "right" person to love, the "right" person to marry. Certain things in life were totally unpredictable; she'd always known that. But she hadn't counted on love fitting into that category.

Just as she hadn't counted on falling in love with the one man who was so completely "wrong" for her; whose career would necessitate their being apart most of the time, and whose outlook on relationships was so entirely different from her own. But she'd just admitted it, hadn't she? Bobbi Ann Morrow was in love with Blain Pearson.

She had been all along, too, hadn't she? Oh, how Mary Beth would gloat if she could hear all this, she mused wryly. Determined to plan her entire life, including the most intimate yearnings of her heart's desire, she had miscalculated the fact that love wasn't necessarily something one could plan on.

It was a cruel admission, especially then, considering the futility of it all. Even if she *was* willing to make a few changes in her life to accommodate the man she loved, there was nothing she could do about it. A vision of Blain's disgusted face staring down at her flitted into her brain and she shuddered both inwardly and outwardly. His emotional reaction to seeing Ralph in her apartment was what had surprised her so. Perhaps he did care for her more than she'd assumed. Well, so what? The observation was merely academic at that point anyway.

Reaching down, Bobbi turned up the cold water till the hot couldn't be felt anymore. She soaped herself vigorously, almost bruisingly, as if the action could somehow purge her of her stupidity.

Bobbi went through the motions of living the next week in robotlike fashion. It was an effort to go out with the crowd at work for lunch, but she did so, as much to appear as normal as possible as to immerse herself in enough outside stimulation to overcome her miserable thoughts.

But there was no escaping them when nighttime came and she was alone again. The solitude that had once been a symbol of her self-sufficiency engulfed her in a fearsome loneliness. Was she to live that way the rest of her life? She honestly didn't think she could stand it. Almost everything in the apartment reminded her of Blain and the time he'd spent there. Her mind told her she would meet someone else and the memories would fade, but her heart couldn't accept it—had no desire to accept it.

By Friday she was wondering how she was going to make it until Monday. Work had never looked so good; at least it kept her from going completely crazy. By Saturday she was wishing she had made plans— any plans—just to have something to do. She called Mary Beth, who hadn't called all week long. She supposed the girl had had enough of her lunacy the previous week. She would apologize for her behavior and get things on the right track with her friend.

But Mary Beth wasn't home. She had left her answering machine on, and as much as Bobbi disliked talking to the silly thing, she left a message anyway.

After putting in a call to her parents, the sound of her mother's voice providing a soothing measure of care and warmth, Bobbi busied herself turning the apartment topsy-turvy, giving it the spring cleaning she had been putting off for too long. By early afternoon she still hadn't received a return call from Mary Beth and she resigned herself to a solitary luncheon. She had intended to offer to pick up Mary Beth's favorite pizza for the two of them to share, but it wasn't worth the effort for only herself.

Removing the scarf that had held back her hair, she shook the tresses loose and wiped her damp neck with the tail of her oversize T-shirt, which hung to the bottom edge of her faded cut-offs. She had skipped breakfast that morning—as she had most every morning as of late—and after all the exertion, her hunger pains were increasing rapidly. Walking through the living room, she switched on the television and continued on into the kitchen, not bothering to see what particular program was on.

She prepared a grilled cheese sandwich and poured a glass of cold milk, placed them on a tray, and carried it into the living room. Only after she sat down and quenched her thirst with a gulp of the milk, did she turn her attention to the sports program in progress on the television.

Her hand, which was holding the grilled cheese sandwich, froze halfway to her mouth as she listened to the two commentators discussing the first half of a basketball game. The second half was about to begin, and her jaw slackened visibly as she heard Blain's name being brought up repeatedly. Placing the sandwich back on the plate, she sat up straighter, listening carefully to every word being said.

"Pearson's had quite a career," one commentator quipped. "The Bullets will have a hard time replacing his position as guard with another of such expertise and talent."

"I agree with you there, Bob. Or as much experience. I'll have to say I was surprised as most fans when he announced that this is his last season. Of course he was under an open-ended contract—there was nothing mysterious about that—but he made absolutely no mention whatsoever to the press of his plans."

"I'm sure the other team members hate to see him

go too, Dick. But this game is a hot one for both teams today. At this point I can't see any way of predicting what turn the last half is going to take, can you?''

"No, Bob, I can't. The Celtics are behind by six points, but there's no telling..."

Bobbi reached slowly for the sandwich, but it was tasteless as she bit into it, chewing automatically. Blain was retiring from professional basketball! She couldn't believe her ears. Why had he never mentioned it before? she wondered. Surely he had not decided something so momentous overnight. But then, he'd kept it such a secret from everyone else, why would he have wanted to discuss it with her?

Unless, of course, *that* was what he meant when he said he wanted to talk to her about something. Could it have been that? Her heart skipped a beat at the thought and her hand shook as she reached for the glass of milk and lifted it to her lips, gulping it down in spasmodic nervousness.

The telephone rang just then, and she started to get up and answer it, but the television camera zoomed in on the court, focusing for a few seconds on Blain as he stood mingling with his teammates. The ring of the phone and the comments of the sportscasters were a blur to Bobbi as she sat transfixed. It was as though he were there in that very room. A close-up shot revealed in almost intimate detail what she had unsuccessfully erased from memory. Her gaze was drawn to the picture of him like a magnet to metal, and she studied every centimeter of his face with an intensity born of physical hunger.

The penetrating blue eyes; the hard, angular planes of his face; the abundant auburn hair, lightly curling at his nape. Her hands clutched in response, her fingers aching to reach through the screen, to touch him, caress him...

She shifted on the couch, her eyes never leaving the television, but as she moved her hands to her side one touched the remote control device that lay beside her. She picked it up and brought it in front of her. Absently she stroked it, her gaze following every movement on the screen, riveting on Blain's whirling, darting figure every time it came within the camera's angle.

The beat of her heart had taken up a ridiculous tempo; it was as if he were another Blain Pearson. The *real* Blain Pearson. In a crazy fantasy she imagined him stopping in his tracks right there on court, looking through the camera lens and into her living room, directly at her. What would she say to him? Come back? Please, come back. I need to talk to you, to hold you again, to admit how much I need...

Reason told her she should turn off the damn set, relieve herself of the agony of seeing him that way. But her heart stayed the hand that would have pressed the off button. She had to see him—in any way possible.

She watched the rest of the game, memorizing every move Blain made on the court. She knew so little of the sport, but it was clear even to her unfamiliar mind that he was indeed a brilliantly talented athlete; gone was the image of the dumb jock she had stereotyped him as being. There was far, far more depth to the man; she knew that now.

Sitting as rigid as if she were made of wood, Bobbi turned the volume up and listened to the running commentary of the sportscasters. The feeling she had experienced when she'd gone to the game at the Capital Centre flooded over her, raising goose bumps of excitement on her flesh in much the same way she had responded then. She remembered her initial impression of how incredible it was that so many bodies, whirling and careening around one another, managed to keep from colliding with one another full force.

Then, as she watched in amazed horror, her fears became reality as the noise and tension spiraled furiously, and during a frantic attempt by the Bullets to score, the players beneath the basket bunched together and slammed against one another. One of the players was knocked to the floor during the scramble, his body twisting awkwardly as he slid for a few feet before stopping in a crumpled heap.

Bobbi felt her stomach sink sickeningly as the auburn head moved and the camera caught a brief look of agony twisting the familiar features.

Instinctively her hand went to her throat as she listened in shocked disbelief to the sportscasters. But their gibberish went unheeded as she gazed wildly at the screen. He couldn't get up! A crowd of players and medical aides had gathered around Blain as he lay back on the floor, their bodies blocking from view what was taking place. Infuriatingly a commercial broke in, and Bobbi pounded a fist in agitation on the couch. When the regular program resumed a full minute and a half later, the game was in progress once more and Blain was obviously not on the court. Bobbi listened intently, and it was finally revealed that Pearson *had* been injured, perhaps seriously, and was being taken to a hospital. Bobbi's frustration mounted as the two commentators discussed the unfortunate circumstances of Blain Pearson's last professional game. Hopefully he would...

Bobbi stood and punched viciously at the remote control device, turning the set off. She didn't need to hear that sentimental garbage! Blain was injured, that's all that mattered. She needed to do something! More than anything in her life she needed to know what was happening to him. If she had thought her heartbeat too rapid before, it was going absolutely berserk at the moment. The memory of his agonized features plastered across her brain seared her with an agony of her own.

Erratically she paced the floor of the apartment, crossing from living room to kitchen and back again, picking up the tray containing her barely eaten lunch and carrying it to the kitchen sink. Turning on the water, she began rinsing out the glass.

To hell with this! she thought, jerking off the faucet and walking back into the living room, picking up the receiver of the telephone. She punched Mary Beth's number quickly, hoping the damn answering device wasn't all she'd hear.

"Hello?"

"Mary Beth," Bobbi said breathlessly. "You're home."

"Yeah, I got your message. I called you a while ago, but—"

"I need your help," Bobbi cut in, praying Mary Beth was the friend she had always been, hoping she'd forgotten or forgiven Bobbi's bitchy behavior last week. "Oh, Mary Beth, I'm so worried."

"What's wrong," Mary Beth asked in a concerned tone. "Are you all right?"

"No. Yes— I mean, I'm fine. It's Blain. He's been hurt, and I don't know what to do. Or if there *is* anything to do."

Mary Beth hesitated, frowning in consternation at what she thought she had just heard. When had *he* entered the picture again? she wondered. But she and Bobbi hadn't talked all week long. Evidently *something* had happened, but whatever it was she really didn't need to know. Her seldom-failing intuition told her that somehow, for some reason, Bobbi had finally come to her senses.

"All right. Tell me what happened," Mary Beth said calmly. She listened as Bobbi related in a rush what she had just seen on television. She didn't ask any unnecessary questions, only advised Bobbi to relax and hang on for a few minutes. She would see what she could do and be over as soon as possible.

Bobbi didn't have to wait long; Mary Beth was knocking on her door within half an hour.

"All right, here's what you're gonna do," Mary Beth said as she walked into the room, dressed in a pair of Levi's jeans and a gray sweat shirt, her brown hair pulled into a pony tail.

Bobbi stared at her wide-eyed, like a little girl ready to obey her mother's orders. Mary Beth faced her squarely, her legs apart and her hands on her hips as she spoke. "Don't ask me how I did it. I have a *very* good friend in Boston—she works in medical records at Boston General—anyway, she found out the name of the hospital they brought Blain to. If you hurry, I can take you to Dulles to catch a flight into Logan. It leaves at three thirty. That gives you an hour and a half. You can rent a car at the airport and drive to the hospital."

"How did you find out about the flight?"

Mary Beth shrugged. "Simple. I called. I also made a reservation for you."

Bobbi's eyes grew watery and a lump formed in her throat as she stared at her friend. Impulsively she reached out and embraced Mary Beth, muttering chokingly, "Oh, Mary Beth, how can I ever thank you?" She pulled back and peered at her friend sheepishly. "Forgive me for my stupidity and rudeness last week."

Mary Beth shook her head, sending the pony tail bobbing from side to side. "Don't be ridiculous. All of us go through periods of mental illness occasionally."

Bobbi laughed. "Oh, Mary Beth, you're nuts!"

"I know, and you're gonna be late if you don't hurry up."

"Right." Bobbi composed herself and rushed out of the room, flinging the bedroom door against the wall in her hurry.

Mary Beth's brown eyes glinted knowingly as she watched Bobbi hurry out of the room to pack. She had been right from the beginning; she'd never seen an individual more in love than Bobbi Morrow.

Bobbi waited impatiently at the nurse's station. There had just been a change of shifts, and she was reluctant to intrude at the moment. She sat on a padded bench next to the elevators and nervously squeezed the leather material of her purse. Finally it looked as though the situation at the nurse's station was under control, and she approached the desk.

"Excuse me," she said softly through the opening in the glass partition separating the wide desk from the corridor.

A middle-aged nurse looked up from the chart she was scribbling in and asked, "Yes, may I help you?"

Bobbi cleared her throat and answered hoarsely, "Uh, yes... I would like to know which room Mr. Blain Pearson is in. The information desk told me he was on the third floor, but there was no room number available."

"Mr. Pearson is under strict no-visitors orders at this time."

Bobbi's heart plummeted. To have gone all that way and— No! She was not going to be a baby about it. "But—but I've come a long way and—"

"I'm sorry, miss, but there's nothing I can do about it. Doctor's orders. Perhaps you can try again in the morning."

Bobbi bit her tongue and turned away from the unconcerned nurse. What was she going to do now? Go sneaking down the hall peeking into rooms until she found him and then have a nurse come in and throw her out? No, that wasn't the way she wanted to see him at all. Her stomach growled audibly just then and she decided it would perhaps be wiser to have something to eat in the cafeteria and then decide what to do.

As it turned out she spent the most uncomfortable night she could ever recall in her entire life, sleeping in a half-reclining position on a vinyl chair in one of the hospital's waiting lounges. But the nurse in Station Three that morning agreed that even though it was early, Bobbi could go in and see Mr. Pearson, since she was a member of the family. Bobbi had told the little white lie in a most convincing tone, rather pleased with her newly discovered acting ability.

"He's been receiving medication around the clock for the pain," the nurse explained as she walked with Bobbi down the hall to Blain's room, "but perhaps company will take his mind off it for a while."

Bobbi smiled graciously. "Perhaps it will."

She stood just outside the door as the nurse knocked once and peeked in when Blain growled his response.

"Mr. Pearson, you have a visitor," she said warmly, opening the door wider. "Your sister is here."

"My wha—" Blain, whose face was heavily shadowed by a day and a half's growth of beard, was scowling much like he had when he'd stalked away from her apartment.

"Hello, Blain," Bobbi said softly, stepping tentatively into the room.

The scowl never left Blain's face, but Bobbi thought she detected some sort of light in those ocean-blue eyes.

Sardonically he cocked one dark eyebrow. "Sister?"

Bobbi smiled, a vain attempt to disguise the nervousness racking her insides. He would have to be blind not to see she was shaking like a leaf. "It was the only way I could think of to get them to let me see you this early," she explained, moving closer to the bed but keeping a respectful distance from the foot of it. "After last night, I didn't exactly care to be told again to come back later."

"What do you mean, 'after last night'?"

Bobbi licked her lips distractedly and felt a hot flush stain her cheeks. She cleared her throat. "I tried to see you last night, but the night nurse wouldn't let me," she explained.

Both dark eyebrows shot up as Blain asked, "You were here last night? In the hospital?"

Bobbi lowered her eyes and gave a barely perceptible nod.

"Where did you stay? How did you get to Boston? And why did you come?"

That last question stung, but Bobbi forced down the reaction it produced. Determinedly she sat down on the edge of a visitor's chair near the bed, placing her purse primly on her lap. She stared at the floor for a moment, then lifted her gaze to meet his. "I came because I wanted to see how you were. To see if you were all right."

"Why?" Blain questioned harshly.

"Be-because I saw you get hurt and—and I was worried."

"I'm touched," he mumbled, grunting as he shifted his weight and moved his injured leg.

Bobbi looked at him in alarm. "Are you all right?"

"Of course I'm all right." Blain gritted out the words sarcastically. "Why else would I be lying in a hospital bed with a screwed-up hamstring?"

Again Bobbi's cheeks flushed in embarrassment. "I meant, do you want me to call the nurse for you?"

Blain lifted the small control device attached to the wall via a long cord. "If I want the nurse, I can have her here in a second with this."

Bobbi looked away. She was getting nowhere fast in this conversation. She had not gone there for a verbal sparring match. Of course, she hadn't imagined a nice, amiable conversation between the two of them, but neither had she thought she'd get that hostile a reception either.

"Blain, I came here to see you because I—"

"Because you what?" Blain's glare pierced right through her, and it took every ounce of resolve that Bobbi had to continue on with what she felt inside but had not given any thought as to how to put into words.

She drew in a deep breath. "Because I wanted to tell you I'm sorry about last weekend."

"Why?" Blain asked bluntly. "You have nothing to explain to me, and nothing to be sorry about."

"That's not true." The words rushed out of Bobbi's mouth. "What you saw..." She hesitated, unsure of the proper phrasing of what she meant to say.

"What I saw was all I needed to see. By the way, where is he tonight?"

"Who?"

Blain emitted a gruff sound somewhere between a laugh and a derisive scoff. "Lover boy."

Bobbi frowned, truly stunned by the degree of jealousy evident in Blain's tone. "Ralph is not my lover," she stated quietly.

"Ralph, is it?" Blain rolled his eyes upward. "Such a romantic name."

"Who cares about his name?" Bobbi retorted, anger building then with his silly reaction. She hadn't been prepared for it. "Ralph is a man I work with at AMAC. He was at my apartment Saturday night to celebrate a promotion he got."

"Some celebration," Blain muttered disbelievingly.

Bobbi sighed exasperatedly. "Look, this is ridiculous. I came here to explain to you why I was so...what was really going on."

Blain crossed his arms over his chest and shrugged disinterestedly, as if whatever she had to say made no difference anyway. "Yes?"

Bobbi's eyes scanned the room, finally coming to rest on Blain's formidable features once more. "Ralph was at my apartment to celebrate something else besides his promotion. His engagement. He's getting married to a girl he went to college with."

Blain pursed his lips and nodded knowingly. "Uh-huh. And he came to you for one last fling before taking the plunge."

Angry sparks flared within Bobbi then, and she thrust her purse down on the chair next to her. "*No,* he didn't come to me for a last fling," she hurled at him. "He's a very good friend, that's all. We've known each other for a long time, and he wanted to share the news with me before anyone else. And," she went on, moving slowly toward the bed, her initial reticence thoroughly overcome now, "this conversation is absolutely ridiculous. I came to see you because I watched you get hurt on television. I was worried to death that it might be serious, Blain Pearson. I'm beginning to think I should be sorry I came now."

Blain's eyes narrowed cautiously. "All right. So you were concerned about my injury. But why all the sudden sympathy? You couldn't have cared less about answering my phone calls. I got pretty damn tired of hearing the damn thing slammed in my ear these past couple of weeks."

"Oh, really?" Bobbi snapped, placing one hand on her hip and cocking her head to the side. "Well, I'm real sorry about that, but I wasn't in the mood for any of your phony excuses."

"Excuses?"

"Come on. Don't play the innocent bit now, Blain. Who was she? One of the regulars, or a new one you picked up for the weekend? Like you did with me," she added bitterly.

Blain squinted and his expression hardened. "Maybe if you would have listened, you wouldn't be sounding like such a fool right now."

Bobbi's eyes widened and she jabbed a thumb at her breastbone. "Me a fool! Let me tell you something, Mr.—"

"Oh, shut up," he growled, reaching out swiftly and pulling her onto the bed next to him. Bobbi flushed as her eyes traveled downward, following the sheet, which had dropped to just below his bare waistline..

"You always have been too big for your britches, so you're gonna keep your trap shut and listen to me. Like you should have a long time ago."

Bobbi frowned and bit her lower lip, subdued for the moment.

"Now, I'm not gonna say this but once," Blain said sternly, loosening his hold on her elbow now that she appeared to be sitting still, "so you better listen up.

"First of all, the woman who answered the phone the night you called me in L.A. was a friend's sister-in-law, to whom I happened to give a ride and who happened to invite herself up to my room. And," he added dryly, "who was sent packing the minute she hung up and gave me your message." Suddenly his anger resurfaced toward the pushy broad; if she had been a man, he would have decked her. His visions of temporary companionship that evening had fizzled the minute she'd gotten in the car with him. She'd been an unbearable bore, and he'd been incredibly stupid to even let her go up to his room. He still couldn't figure out why he'd done it.

"She was nothing. Period." He paused, and when he spoke, his voice was lower, quieter.

"I had something important to discuss with you the day you were entertaining...Ralph."

Bobbi looked up at him expectantly.

"I wanted to get your opinion on a couple of university coaching positions I've been offered."

"You did?" She couldn't help the surprise in her tone.

Blain's Adam's apple rose and fell, and he studied

the calling device he was still clutching as if to analyze its entire construction. "I wanted to know which one you would prefer."

He said it so quietly, Bobbi wasn't at all sure she had heard correctly. Her heart was certainly being put through its paces that night, from fairly halting to the rapid tattoo she was sure was bordering on fibrillation. Thank God she was in a hospital.

"What difference would my opinion make?" she asked, trying desperately to stop the shivering that had started again in her rib cage. She felt hot and cold at the same time.

Blain looked up then and the expression in his eyes was as different from the one that had initially greeted her as night and day. A mixture of hurt and fear and hope swirled within those cerulean-blue irises, and Bobbi's crazed heart leaped in anticipation.

"I don't want to make a fool of myself, Bobbi," he said huskily. "I hope to God you didn't just come here tonight on some mission of mercy because you felt sorry for me."

"Oh, Blain, no..."

He waved aside the objection. "Because if you did, you can walk out that door right now."

Bobbi blinked, not moving an inch.

Blain continued. "I know we haven't had much time together. But what we have shared has been good. Real good. I've always been a man who made up my mind about things pretty quickly once I was sure that was what I wanted. And I never look back. I've never had cause to regret that particular philosophy." He hesitated and drew in a deep breath that made his chest expand. It was all Bobbi could do to keep from laying her head against it.

"What I'm trying to say— What I meant to say to you the night you sent me away, Bobbi, was that I think it could work between us. Marriage. Sharing a life together."

Bobbi's heart strained beyond measure then as his words hit her full force. She felt whisked out of the present just then, as if she were floating on a different dimension of awareness. But it was a glorious sensation, keeping her from doing the one thing that surely would get her kicked out of the room—shouting at the top of her lungs!

"Oh, Blain," she breathed as she reached out and took one of his hands in both her own. "I can't believe you're actually saying this."

Her green eyes now held only hope, and a slow smile began spreading his full, sensuous lips, which she had possessed before and longed for with all her heart that very moment. "But I am," he whispered, reaching out with his other hand to pull her down toward him.

Bobbi angled her body more closely against him, hoping a nurse didn't arrive too soon to ask her to leave. Blain placed a hand at the nape of her neck, crushing her cinnamon-colored hair and pulling her head down lower to his own. "I'm waiting," he said, his gaze moving from her eyes to her slightly parted lips and back again.

"Waiting for what?" Bobbi whispered back, aching to taste his lips.

His hand tightened around her nape as he demanded, "For your answer. Will you be my wife? Follow me to the ends of the earth; love, cherish, and honor me till death do us part?" The loving sparkle in his eyes was contagious.

Bobbi wanted to laugh, to spin around in joyous circles, to kiss the lips so near her own. But she drew back a bit and feigned a confused, concerned expression. "Am I to understand that you love me, Blain Pearson?"

"Of course I love you," he muttered thickly, his lips hovering next to hers.

"Oh, Blain, I love you, too. I think I did from the beginning. And, yes"—her lips brushed lightly against his—"yes, I'll marry you. I'd be a fool not to."

And a fool she'd been for far too long already, she mused silently, relishing the sweet, perfect taste of the mouth she would always claim solely for her own.

Chapter Sixteen

Bobbi stood on the veranda of the old Victorian-style house and waved back and forth, sniffing loudly as tears of nostalgia misted her vision. Mary Beth waved back one last time, then drove off down the maple-lined street.

Bobbi smiled then, thinking back over how much she and Blain had enjoyed Mary Beth's visit. She felt a familiar movement within and grinned as she rested her hand atop her swollen belly. Well, she'd see her again soon enough. As soon as little Bucko decided to make his eagerly-awaited appearance.

"Well, I can't stand here all day," she muttered aloud, almost knocking over a can of paint as she turned to go back inside. Painting was Blain's project, thank God. She'd do anything else she could but paint!

But Blain didn't mind. In fact, he was good at it. He was really enjoying himself, getting the old rambling estate fixed up. Just as he enjoyed their more subdued life-style here in Raleigh, where he'd accepted the head coach position at the university. Blain had gotten his wish last year; he'd recovered rapidly from the injured hamstring and had gone on to play with the team in the play-offs. The Bullets had captured the championship, and Blain wore his championship ring constantly, a cherished memento of the life he'd led so fully and so happily until settling down had become the more important factor.

And Bobbi was thrilled to share that new phase of his life...their life. The first year of their marriage had been fun, exciting, relaxing. Now she was looking forward to the addition to the Pearson household as much as her husband.

An hour later she was squatting next to an enormous birch tree on the front lawn as she tended the flower bed encircling it. She heard his footsteps on the sidewalk, but her coordination was becoming increasingly clumsy of late and she wasn't able to stand before Blain crossed the yard and stood next to her.

His hands encircled her waist as he helped pull her up, drawing her close to him as he bent to kiss the top of her head. "Mmmm, you smell good," he teased, grinning down at her.

"Blain, that's not fair! I've been out here for a solid hour—in the sun!—making sure my plants are gonna make it."

"I was just teasing." He placed one hand on her stomach. "How's he doing?"

"'He' doesn't like gardening very much." Bobbi smirked. "I've been getting the daylights kicked out of me." Blain glanced over Bobbi's shoulder at the green sprouts just peeking out of the soil. "What are they?"

"Daisies, of course," she admonished lightly.

He cocked an eyebrow and glanced at her questioningly, then a dawning light appeared within the azure depths of his eyes. "That bouquet last year...you haven't forgotten, have you?"

Bobbi moved as close to him as her rounded stomach would allow and nuzzled her cheek against his chest. "How could I forget the most beautiful flowers anyone ever gave me?" She glanced up at him, her green eyes shining moistly. "Now I can have as many as I want...whenever I want."

Blain smiled and bent his lanky frame, lowering his dark auburn head to plant a kiss of approval on her softly parted lips.

Enter a uniquely exciting new world with

Harlequin American Romance ™·

Harlequin American Romances are the first romances to explore today's love relationships. These compelling novels reach into the hearts and minds of women across America... probing the most intimate moments of romance, love and desire.

You'll follow romantic heroines and irresistible men as they boldly face confusing choices. Career first, love later? Love without marriage? Long-distance relationships? All the experiences that make love real are captured in the tender, loving pages of Harlequin American Romances.

What makes American women so different when it comes to love? Find out with Harlequin American Romance!

Send for your introductory FREE book now!

Get this book FREE!

Yours FREE, with a home subscription to SUPERROMANCE™

Now you never have to miss reading the newest **SUPERROMANCES**… because they'll be delivered right to your door.

Start with your **FREE** LOVE BEYOND DESIRE. You'll be enthralled by this powerful love story…from the moment Robin meets the dark, handsome Carlos and finds herself involved in the jealousies, bitterness and secret passions of the Lopez family. Where her own forbidden love threatens to shatter her life.

Your **FREE** LOVE BEYOND DESIRE is only the beginning. A subscription to **SUPERROMANCE** lets you look forward to a long love affair. Month after month, you'll receive four love stories of heroic dimension. Novels that will involve you in spellbinding intrigue, forbidden love and fiery passions.

You'll begin this series of sensuous, exciting contemporary novels…written by some of the top romance novelists of the day…with four every month.

And this big value…each novel, almost 400 pages of compelling reading…is yours for only $2.50 a book. Hours of entertainment every month for so little. Far less than a first-run movie or pay-TV. Newly published novels, with beautifully illustrated covers, filled with page after page of delicious escape into a world of romantic love…delivered right to your home.

Begin a long love affair with
SUPERROMANCE.
Accept LOVE BEYOND DESIRE **FREE.**

Complete and mail the coupon below today!

- -

FREE!   Mail to: SUPERROMANCE

In the U.S.
2504 West Southern Avenue
Tempe, AZ 85282

In Canada
649 Ontario St.
Stratford, Ontario N5A 6W2

YES, please send me FREE and without any obligation, my
SUPERROMANCE novel, LOVE BEYOND DESIRE. If you do not hear
from me after I have examined my FREE book, please send me the
4 new **SUPERROMANCE** books every month as soon as they come
off the press. I understand that I will be billed only $2.50 for each book
(total $10.00). There are no shipping and handling or any other hidden
charges. There is no minimum number of books that I have to
purchase. In fact, I may cancel this arrangement at any time.
LOVE BEYOND DESIRE is mine to keep as a FREE gift, even if
I do not buy any additional books.

NAME _____ (Please Print) _____

ADDRESS _____ APT. NO. _____

CITY _____

STATE/PROV. _____ ZIP/POSTAL CODE _____

SIGNATURE (If under 18, parent or guardian must sign.) _____

134-BPS-XAFN

This offer is limited to one order per household and not valid to present
subscribers. Prices subject to change without notice. **Offer expires March 31, 1984**